CONNECTING THE DOTS IN OUR UNIVERSE

Gary Stokes

Gary Stokes/ Publisher

Connecting the Dots In Our Universe/ Gary Stokes. -- 1st ed.
ISBN 978-1-7335206-0-7

Dedicated to my wife Carolyn Stokes who is my muse, my editor, and my technical support. Thank you, Carolyn. Without your many, many hours of work this book would not have been possible.

CONTENTS

INTRODUCTION

Why did I write this book? When the December 21, 2012 predicted destruction did not happen it upset me so severely that I wrote this book and had to dig deeper and deeper to find out just what happened. This is my attempt to answer questions about the 2012 anomaly and other anomalies and events in nature and life as I see them. To seek the truth by going to the essence. To go to the center and work outward.

Remember the 1950s toy, the Magic 8 Ball™? You asked the ball a yes-no type of question. Then you flipped the ball over and a triangle appeared on the bottom with your answer. In a way, this book, *Connecting the Dots In Our Universe*, is the Magic 8 Ball™ of the essence of life.

All my life has been about asking questions and searching for the answers to those questions. Questions about extraterrestrials, Yin and Yang, good and evil. Questions about why the predicted devastation on December 21, 2012 did not happen. Questions about the creation of the sun, the planets, the Earth, the moon, Mars and the fifth planet or asteroid belt. Questions even about DNA, the essence of life. From the beginning to the end in connecting the dots in our universe.

Connecting the Dots in Our Universe is my take on the answers to these questions. I am not a scientist but I am a thinker who seeks the truth. These are my theories that I have developed over a time of study.

CHAPTER ONE

THE EXTRATERRESTRIALS

Why Are They Here?

Who are the extraterrestrials? The extraterrestrials or aliens as they are sometimes called are intelligent beings from another life that came to planet Earth in an earlier time. These beings influenced the development of our planet and our society. Where did they come from? Why did they come to planet Earth? And most important of all, what are they doing here?

When people talk about the extraterrestrials they always talk about them being gray or white, this tall or this short, right? But nobody ever mentions if their genitalia are exposed or if they are wearing clothes. Is this just the image they project for us to see? Is their genitalia exposed that they don't cover up? Do they even have any gender? Why do they not wear clothes? What facial features and what body features do they have? Why do we always say that they are gray? In other words what do they really look like?

4 · GARY STOKES

Where did the extraterrestrials live before they came to planet Earth? Why did they leave their planet and come to the planet Earth? They had to leave their planet where they were because they destroyed it. One reason could be that contamination or disease made them leave their planet. That might have been what made them turn into the color they are. The planet that they were on was contaminated for one reason or another. Or they could have been in some type of warring situation that contaminated their planet. Radioactivity could also have contaminated their planet.

I believe that their planet became infected with something that the extraterrestrials released to kill off all the inhabitants on their planet. Most likely it was a science project that went wrong that caused the end of their own extinction. Can you imagine the guilt that this might have caused? A whole civilization was wiped out. A science experiment that went wrong and you had to kill off everything that had the bacteria, the disease.

Their planet could have been naturally destroyed by a planetary wide disease which destroyed all of their DNA most likely and made them where they could not reproduce and continue their science experiments. The only logical point of view for all of them to have been removed would be for food or to be relocated or a medical situation which had to be eradicated. Why would you leave the planet unless you ran out of water or something that basic? What is the real essence basic reason of why their planet was evacuated or sterilized or whatever you want to call it?

Or was it a DNA mistake that caused them to have to leave their planet and come to planet Earth? They had to start the gene pool all over for a fresh new one like the one they had created before. They might be creating a fresh gene pool on planet Earth right now. They are trying to recreate their own essence as it was hundreds or thousands of years before.

We were already here on the planet Earth. The planet was already replicated here and ready to be inhabited by them. But as you and I know, they had to recreate the planet where they were here on planet Earth so they would have a place to stay. I think that we were just a civilization that they brought with them to use as a science experiment. We are no less than the human genome of normality or clone DNA and from there they changed all the different functions and structures of it.

The extraterrestrials were basically refugees from space when they came to planet Earth after the destruction and demise of their planet. Therefore, our planet was accepting refugees way before America even became America. So here again lies the rub of how conscious we were and how this was a situation of them not having a place to go. We shared the planet with them. But it cost them because they had to educate the people on the planet until they became good enough to protect themselves on their own. Now here again this shows you that the planet Earth has always been a place that accepts refugees.

They say that we were created in their own image. Where is the reality of saying that we were here before they came? Nothing. There is no way to prove it. So, if that is the case then logically what I am saying is correct.

See if you do not pay attention then you would continue to think that the planet Earth was already here before they came and created it. You would never know that we were a science experiment but just another life form that just happened by and decided to have a perfect "Goldilocks Zone" that was just left and then have it even though there are how many of them looking for a place to live.

Ask yourself the overseeing extraterrestrials' point of view that we have here to explain. Would they not control you with sound waves if they had a way to? It is quite logical they had a way at the time. They can release the button and there are no more sound waves. Possibly the true one hundred percent ability of your brain will be at least accessible to those who are trying to get through the maze and those who are not will be stuck in a puddle. You always think you can turn water into cream but it will not even happen. It is still just water.

Why would you leave the planet where you live? What would be the reason? Why did they come here? Maybe the reason they came here was for the water that was on planet Earth. After all, the real acquisition of wealth and power into the extraterrestrials and all of the people in all of the other solar systems is the amount of water that you have on the planet. This is the vanity of the extraterrestrials. How much water they gathered because it is the most valuable of all resources.

Maybe the only real realization that we have not talked about yet is they came here to extrapolate the minerals out of the planet and all of this other stuff developed from it. They go from planet to planet doing what they can do, inserting a nuclear motor into the planet if they are going to stay there a while, perking the planet, cracking the planet, and fracking the planet to get all the oils and minerals they can from the planet before they go ahead and stick the motor inside so they can heat it up and extrapolate everything that the planet has. Unfortunately for us the planet Earth just happened to be a "Goldilocks" zone which just happened to be a great place to be because it did not get too hot and it did not get too cold. So here again think of the simplicity of all this but yet the time it takes to become a space explorer. Imagine going to a planet or an asteroid or something like that, that you can heat it up and then you can extrapolate from it and how many thousands of years does that take in the future with our technologies for you and me to think this.

Maybe this time they stopped themselves before they totally destroyed the planet. In other words, they might have caught themselves from destroying the planet Earth here like they had done before on the other planet. In other words, they might have realized all the problems that caused them to explode Mars and the asteroid belt planet. Maybe this time they stopped themselves from total obliteration again on planet Earth and that is what they are doing here now. They destroyed Mars and the asteroid planet and here again the same Yin and Yang brothers might have come close to doing the same thing here again. Who knows, maybe they achieved their goal and maybe they didn't. Maybe it is a science project that they are trying to figure out as it goes on and on until we get there. Maybe they have nothing else to do or it is the last question they have to ask. We don't know because we are not there yet.

So to go along with this, remember the explorer Admiral Byrd? When he flew over Antarctica, he saw an opening that went into the inner earth. The opening going down into the base of the Earth there had a nice smooth entryway that was like the opening of a carburetor. This opening could be an opening for the extraterrestrials to be able to live inside the planet Earth. Imagine the same type of opening posted all over the planets that we associate with. Therefore, you could find out if they are living inside the planets. If I was an extraterrestrial where would I go? Evidently, where you cannot find me, right? It just seems logical that if you have these entryways on the planets that would show you that the extraterrestrials live inside the planets instead of on the top side like we do. It would make sense of more security. Here again when you live in a tunnel or a hole, there is only one way in and one way out unless you create an exit.

They have to live inside the planets so they would not get harmed from destruction and things from the outside. And like anybody trying to hide you are only going to have a tunnel entry in one place so that you can hide so nobody else could harm you. It you are still trying to exist with safety, then safety can only exist when no one knows you are around the most part. Agree? You know there is safety in being oneself.

Now if the extraterrestrials could live inside the planet then they could also grow their crops inside the planet. Now did you listen to what I just said? If they can grow crops inside a controlled environment area, they do not need the real sun or anything like it to grow their food. They could basically create their own space time dimension and everything else by making it a dome facility enclosure encapsulation. So basically, they can grow food twenty-four hours a day, seven days a week, and three hundred sixty-five days a year not only on top of the earth but also inside the earth. When you control the sun and the elements you control when it grows and when it blooms. The same thing with us, right?

Why are the extraterrestrials here? Why are they here if they do not have another place to go? Why are they studying us? Why are they allowing us to reproduce at the rate of billions of people laying together every day making more billions of people? Maybe they are here to share with us their information and knowledge. Maybe they are here so they can open up and reestablish DNA and share the growing DNA, a positive growing DNA instead of a dead DNA that cannot reproduce and has become stagnant. Maybe they are dying off and becoming extinct.

A very good possibility of why the extraterrestrials or aliens are around us is the question of their DNA. What if it is the possibility that they are trying to figure out what happened to their DNA which enabled them to be able to reproduce? Maybe they are trying to find out what happened to their original DNA. Or maybe in the process as we study ours they can see and repair theirs. And maybe the situation is one that we have not seen here or studied. What other reason could they be studying our DNA if not to improve or repair their DNA? Or they could be trying to make ours better somehow or to change the DNA structure maybe in the DNA code to locate dormant DNA or how to crack inside the DNA center of it all. They might also be looking for a way to mutate the DNA. I will talk about DNA and extraterrestrials more in the chapter Universe All DNA.

Wouldn't it be funny if the extraterrestrials were trying to change our shape and form to become exactly what they are through more DNA manipulation? Now this could also lead into the point of view of the swirling and the laying together and the producing all the mixed color children in the world to try to find the agenda that they are trying to achieve. But as an interesting point of view, think of it from the other side that the extraterrestrials are trying to make us look more like them or they look more like us.

But here again about my point of view, wouldn't it be funny if the extraterrestrials were going ahead and having unknown sex with these individual women that they took up with them in their spaceships? And the extraterrestrials slowly administer their DNA to the children that they produced with these earth women. Then they start to form it into the society of the world where we live. I say this because I saw a woman on one of the television news programs that had a nose that looked exactly like the nose of an extraterrestrial.

So, I am wondering how many DNAs the extraterrestrials may have sub-seeded into our civilization or our society and our people here to go ahead and make their own selves become the dominant species on the planet, therefore shielding us and pushing us to the side. It is just the process that has to happen. But whole point about the DNA and the extraterrestrials is that you are never going to know all of the answers. You are just going to have to keep an open mind through the doors of thinking about it again and again until you come to the answer.

We are all just a science project. You have to realize and understand the theory of evolution and you just have to understand what we would have become if we would not have been changed by the extraterrestrials. The extraterrestrials who changed our DNA stole our planet so they could take it over. The extraterrestrials that came here stole our planet and changed us from what we would have become to what we are now. They are the ones who made us what we are now.

The Wall of Humanity at Puma Punku in Bolivia has over forty carved stone heads. The heads are of various races or species in addition to some non-human or alien type heads. Why would these figureheads be put there? They are saying "hello" for some reason. Why are they there without us knowing the reason? The stone figureheads on the wall at Puma Punku are there to represent the extraterrestrials' science of their DNA to show that they created all these different species through the DNA that they manufactured. That is another way to look at it.

But I guarantee you that the forty different figureheads on the wall at Puma Punku that brought their DNA here, well they have a place to go back to. So it was that we have these extraterrestrials going back to the different planets to try to resurrect them from being sterile and stuff and this is why they created our planet down here away from them. It was so they would not contaminate planet Earth with the disease that they had on the other planets. Now that would make more sense that they had to go someplace completely different to start a new planet that did not have any disease. So, they had to start a new colony with all forty of these different space people to be able to have a pure place, a pure science lab that was not contaminated on all the other planets. That is why we are here. That is what makes us so unique. So what is also a unique thing with all this is that they came here from Mars and the asteroid belt planet.

In this point of view is that everybody always wonders when the extraterrestrials are going to come back. Maybe they are going to come back when they go through the process of a DNA seeding pool that we are going through by all of us laying together. Is it going to be that long in the future before they come back and pay us a visit? They are supposed to come back, right? Why would you come back before the science project was done?

On the other hand, did the extraterrestrials ever really leave planet Earth? No, they did not. I believe that the extraterrestrials are trapped here on planet Earth until they have educated us enough. The extraterrestrials could not leave here until they had educated us to be able to be educated in the extraterrestrial world of travel.

Who knows maybe the God that the extraterrestrials believed in had written down in his book or Bible that each planet was to be left alone by the inhabitants on the other planets. Therefore, the consequences would be judgmental if you did not do as he said. If the extraterrestrials had a Bible of some nature to guide them and because they messed with us on our planet then they had to educate us and bring us up to standards as the rest of the solar system as well as the rest of cosmic consciousness out in space. This could be as a result of their own destruction of their own home planet. That is why they want to go back home where they originally came from. I understand what a task it is for them to try to do this. You know here again we are just the test subjects that allowed it to happen and we could not defend ourselves at the do as he said. If the extraterrestrials had a Bible of some nature to time. Maybe the extraterrestrials' space God made them sacrifice themselves in order to educate us.

There may be a larger picture for these individuals to have come to our own planet Earth to have changed us into their own image which was the original sin and mistake that made them to have become trapped here on the planet Earth. They could not have gone home because of the sin that they have done. Why did they ever change us in the first place? Why couldn't they have just left us alone and let us mature in our own pattern of existence? That is what I believe is the original sin. That is the reason why they are trapped here in this dimension.

The reason the extraterrestrials are trapped here is because they are the ones that changed our DNA here originally and started the reform or change on the planet before it was originally decided to do. Maybe that is why they had to originally decide to have to come here is because they had exploded the fifth planet that we call the asteroid belt and destroyed Mars so bad that it was uninhabitable and they had to come here. Yes, that is the fact because there is evidence of the nuclear destruction there by the residue left on the surface of Mars. Now we do not know who lived on the asteroid belt planet but we will one day be able to figure it out. Maybe that is what we are doing on this planet now. We are taking the remnants of the people that were alive from that point of view from that planet and bringing them here to this planet here and trying to repopulate and remake their civilization that they destroyed on their planet however many billions of years ago.

Okay, so these guys could not get home through trying to just fly there in their spaceships and they are trapped here in this dimension. I mean look at how many telescopes are pointed up to the stars trying to hear the extraterrestrials talk to us and you are not conscious enough to know that the extraterrestrials fly around and that they could talk to us any time that they wanted to. It is no problem. It is not a matter of extraterrestrials talking to us. It is a matter of the people here on the planet trying to break through and get back to home where they are so they can get away from us and what they basically have got stuck into. Everybody wants to go home for Christmas, don't they? The people have gone home for thousands of years.

A summation or an answer to all of the questions: I believe the reason the extraterrestrials are here is because they destroyed their planet and had to leave it. The planet Earth just happened to be a perfect place because it was not too hot or too cold. Then they changed us and changed our DNA. I think that the original sin is that they are trapped here because they changed our DNA and changed us from what we were supposed to be. We became a science research project for the extraterrestrials.

CHAPTER TWO

THE YIN AND YANG BROTHERS

Two Troublemakers

Remember when you were going to school or any other kind of deal and there were these two different guys or two different girls who were always beating up on each other? They would always be beating on each other, doing this or doing that. Neither one of them would win. They would just always end up being beat up and ratty. In the same way, think about the Yin and Yang brothers as two brothers who are always fighting and who you would want to discipline in your schoolroom. No one would want to be around them or anything like that.

Who are the Yin and Yang brothers? First, I need to explain what yin and yang means. In Chinese philosophy, yin and yang describe two opposite but equal forces that may actually be connected to each other, dependent upon each other, and work together in the natural world. Yin and yang can be thought of as both equal but opposite forces that interact to form a system in which the whole is greater than the parts. Everything has both yin and yang aspects. Yin and yang can symbolize good and evil, light and dark, and so on. Yin and yang are two equal and opposite forces. Even though they may oppose each other, they depend upon each other. You have to have one to have the other. An example of yin and yang as equal but opposite are the Democrat and Republican political parties in the United States today.

The Yin and Yang brothers came to my attention as two troublemakers. We will get to that in just a minute. They are extraterrestrials that are trapped here on planet Earth and are not able to go home. They are trapped here to have to grow us up and be babysitters to us for what they did which is the original sin. Their sin is they changed our DNA to make us in their image to be what they wanted to be in life. Okay, so these guys are trapped here in this dimension and cannot get home by flying there in their spaceships. It is a matter of they are stuck here on the planet and they are trying to break through and get back to their home. Everybody wants to go home for Christmas, don't they? The people have gone home for thousands of years.

What would you do if the Yin and Yang brothers were around you? What would you do? Would you not want to have anything to do with them? Or would you want to just put them out or aside? Of course, you would. Here again lies the reason of why we are where we are now. I believe that the Yin and Yang brothers were cast out from where they lived. Their continual stupidity among the other citizens or their attitude caused them to be kicked out of where they lived. Since they cannot go home, I guess they are going to just make it miserable on the rest of us. That does not make any sense, does it? So anyway, as the case goes on and the Yin and Yang brothers persist. Think of it in that the process even goes farther to the Yin and Yang brothers.

Then the question becomes, what would you do if the Yin and Yang brothers were actually in control of our Universe here? Yes, you heard it. The Yin and Yang brothers are yin and yang or God versus Satan. The Yin and Yang brothers are any two opposing forces that can never win a struggle because of what you would call all the stupidity in this area. But because of the stupidity-ness of not being able to understand neither one of them will ever come out on top. They will destroy themselves and everything else around them. Does this not sound like that is what we are going through here on planet Earth with the good versus evil deal? Does this not sound like these same two brothers?

Look at it this way as if the Yin and Yang brothers are actually God versus Satan or good versus evil. In the Bible you are not supposed to eat from the tree of knowledge of good and evil, right? Yin and Yang, it is a no win scenario type of information that you need to put into you. The extraterrestrials or call them demons force God and Satan to have the conflict between them so they could settle the issues of the yin and yang no win scenario of good versus evil. Because of the Christ-Antichrist conflict of the two brothers that is going on in the world, would they ever be happy? No, because it is a no win scenario.

Remember that there is only two in the number for the Yin and Yang brothers. The number two and not three but the number two. I guess there is just the magic number of two with the Yin and Yang brothers but in understanding the Bible, there seems to be three: Father, Son, and the Holy Ghost. Okay, but the Yin and Yang brothers are only two. One or the other.

Remember this is the Yin and Yang brothers. So, who would want anyone of this nature? Would you want them around you anywhere? I mean because one goes one way and one goes the other way and they can never win. They can never be harmonious or be happy together because they are always at each other's throats such as day and night and vice versa. Such as the moon goes up and the sun goes down and we go around and around. They do not know of prospering or anything harmonious other than just their own selves fighting back and forth between themselves.

Do you have a brother or a sister that you do this to? Okay, just imagine as if it is just a never ending going on process. It has been happening this way for decades, hundreds, thousands of years but they can never learn the lesson. Remember the Yin and Yang brothers and in the Bible that we were told to not eat the fruit from this tree because you do not need to learn this lesson of good and evil or the lesson of the Yin and Yang brothers. It is so consuming that very few people can get that way of thinking. And thinking is the third way of life or existing with pleasure and existence without the Yin and Yang brothers.

So anyway, as the case goes on and the Yin and Yang brothers persist. Think of it in that the process goes even farther with the Yin and Yang brothers. I think that it is a matter of really understanding that the extraterrestrials have never really left here. They live with us as an experiment in the DNA and they live here in the water and also in the ground beneath us. They cannot leave. They have been stalled here and are trapped here because of the destruction that they did to themselves on Mars and the fifth planet which is the asteroid belt planet.

The 2012 anomaly kept the Yin and Yang brothers trapped here because there was not a good versus evil conflict or a Christ Antichrist conflict at that time. How can we be all together so we can have the aliens here on the planet Earth and start the extraterrestrials delivery to our society? All of it seems to be the key. Yin and yang or good versus evil.

As you may well see, there are other things that lead from why the Yin and Yang brothers are here, who put them here, and why they cannot leave us alone. Well, they cannot leave us alone. I believe in part that they did what I call the unforgivable sin. They changed our DNA and they stole our planet. That is what I believe. So, if they changed our DNA and made us into their image, did they not take over the planet where we were living as well? Yes, they did. They transferred themselves from the fifth planet. These two guys demised and beat themselves up so much that they destroyed their own planet. When they destroyed their own planet they had to leave and go someplace else. You call it moving or camping, right?

Think about the realization of the Yin and Yang brothers not being able to go back to the dimension which they came from. The yin and yang situation here is the God versus evil which is nothing more than a no win scenario in which they were kicked out of where they were earlier in their lifetime because of their continual inability to be understanding and grow past this point of stupid consumption. That is all. If you decide to not play the game between good and evil but to just have a chance to be yourself. Do you know how to be your own self and be a solid unit? Your self control is called being yourself and not a parental taping situation that has been caused by your parents.

CHAPTER THREE

UNIVERSE ALL DNA

The Essence of Life

Universal DNA, Universe All DNA. Universal DNA or universe all DNA? Which is it that we are talking about? It is both.

First, what basically is DNA? What do the letters D N A stand for? DNA is short for the big long scientific word deoxyribonucleic acid. DNA is the basic molecule containing the genetic instructions for life. Basically, DNA is the genetic instructions that are used in the growth, development, functioning, and reproduction of all known living organisms.

Rosslyn Chapel which was built in the 1400s in Scotland has a large column or pillar with a representation of the DNA helix on it. How can this be since we did not discover the DNA genome until the 1950s? Where did they get the model for this? How did someone know how to depict a DNA model? This indicates that somehow somebody knew about the DNA helix before scientists did in order to incorporate it in the chapel. This shows the divining indication that extraterrestrials were guiding them as such obvious step stones would be. It is like a painting in a room except you do not really know what it is until you get privy to the information.

The whole question is where did the original DNA come from? Rosslyn Chapel as far as I know has the earliest depiction of the DNA helix in a building. The point I am trying to say here is where did the original DNA come from? Where did originally the DNA come from and the math it takes to make DNA is unbelievable.

What is the **original DNA**? Where did the original DNA come from? Was it Adam and Eve being the first two white people on the planet? Was it Christ coming from the Virgin Mary? What is all this DNA doing here? Why is it here on the planet if it did not come from God? You just have to ask yourself honestly and allow yourself to connect the dots and then you can deal with the real truth of knowing that maybe there is the possibility that there is more than one God who controls the DNA chain and the ruling of it.

When Jesus Christ was born here on Earth, was not that the first implication of the DNA being changed by God's DNA being mixed with the earthlings' DNA and producing an offshoot which carries the DNA? That is how you started infecting the planet and making the DNA in your own image and you become them or they become you. Think about it. You have to realize that they basically seeded the DNA mix and produced from it. So, you have to realize from the point of view that we are formed to be in his image. So that means that they changed us to be somehow in his image or is this just a change of the DNA process? How do you change us to be in their image? Well, you have to change the DNA, right? I think that would be the only way to change the image. So here again is that not starting the manipulation of infecting DNA and everything? How else do you change us into their image without changing the DNA structure through the process of reproduction to bring forth the desired DNA for the complete change or alteration of the specie that was here?

According to the Bible, God created the first two people, Adam and Eve, on the planet Earth. But the Bible does not mention the other people that were also originally on the planet. It does not mention the people of different colors and from the other areas of the planet. The Bible does not cover all the other humans that could have been on the planet at that time. Just that we were here and we are supposed to go forth and populate.

It is just the simplicity and the stupidity of the obvious that keeps the wool pulled over your eyes that allows you to understand there is no way that this earth could ever have been just Adam and Eve. But if there were just white people, then the whole planet should be white and we should all be connected together through the DNA. Right? Okay, and then we know that is impossible because of all the different colors and variations of the species.

Look at it this way, if they just have Adam and Eve on the planet, look at all the different variations they've made to our basic DNA from Adam and Eve into all the different species. I should not say species. Look at all the different colors, all the different visual effects of all the different eyes and noses, and all the differences between all the people. So if we were not populated by a mass of individuals that had different DNA from all the of the other planets which I believe is the truth, then you are telling me we have scientists that took Adam and Eve in the garden of Eden and did science experiments until they changed all their DNA into all these other people. That is a very real possibility. You have to understand that Adam and Eve were the basic clone individuals and then from there they altered their DNA to basically change them from being what they were originally into what the world and the planet is inhabited with now. That would also allow for Adam and Eve to be the original people here.

If we were put here with only two people and then through time they brought forth Christ, was Christ not the point into the DNA chain that gave the Yin and Yang brothers the discipline to finally understand that there might be a third way of thinking? Is that not what God put into the point that maybe you will understand that eating from the tree of knowledge of good and evil was not actually what you were supposed to do but eventually understand that this is what you have to go through in order to learn? Very possibly the reason why Adam and Eve were here as two white participants is nothing more than a contest between these two extraterrestrials to see which of the dominant DNA would end up in winning the planet. Is it a test to see which DNA is the strongest of all?

There is no way the Garden of Eden could only produce white people. So therefore, I am asking the question that with all these other different types of humans on the planet is that the type of person that ended up surfacing on the planet as the best that the planet could come up with? In other words, from the mustering of all the different types of people laying together, were white people the ones that were the pure universe all DNA strain? It makes you wonder about these individuals that are around that the prominent DNA will be mixed or come to being to produce the next new cycle of human existence.

So, there are all these different people on all these different planets and each planet had a God and each planet had a Christ. Then all these different people lay together to produce all the different types of humans that came to be here on planet Earth itself now. After all these different types of individual and types of DNA differences which ones will rise and be the cream of the crop and be the dominant DNA style of human on the planet now? It will take a while but think of how many times this had to happen.

I am not a scientist. I am just trying to really understand that there is something out there with all of this and trying to make sense of all of it. I am not against religion. I am just asking questions. Obviously, the wool has to be over our eyes because if there was only Adam and Eve here, then there would be only white people on the Earth. So, this is another indication that the extraterrestrials came here. Somebody had to get here or somehow or some way had to make these different looking people. They had to show up somehow so all these different looking people were coming here to visit the planet or to have these people fix the planet when they did come here. There are all these unanswered questions.

We know that there was more than one type of DNA on the planet Earth and there might have been a time in which the white people that God put here were the only DNA on the planet. Each one of the extraterrestrials has proven to you and should prove to you that they are gods to us. If they know DNA so well and so much, what I have asked you to understand about the pure picture of what a DNA would be like before it had any intermixing or interbreeding. What could be the real answer?

Now that you realize that there are more than one species of people on the planet you have to ask yourself, why are there so many species and where did these species come from? Well, it is inevitable that if all the different colors of people are laid together to come up with the universe all DNA which is the color white. Black is the absence of all color in the color chart. White is the blending of all of the colors and is a combination of all. This leads me to believe the universe all DNA to be a one color world eventually. And when it gets to that one color world, is it not the product that they want? They bring in the magic flood again and flood us out and turn the earth or make the earth pivot just a little bit where they drown everybody. Maybe when you get to a pure white color base for all DNA on the planet it becomes extinct and we cannot produce any more children because we are like the seeds. We lose the ability to reproduce because the seed dies off. To be reproductive is no longer allowed or cannot happen or produces mutants.

What is the point of having all of these different people laying together and making all of these different colors of people? Well, it will eventually end up or deduce down to what we call the one world color. In other words, races would be eliminated. If they all laid together at one time then eventually they would end up being one color which would be white. White is the combination or accumulation of all colors. Wait a minute, black is the absence of all the colors and white is the accumulation of all of the colors. So it makes you wonder if everybody laid together and mixed together then you would have a one worldwide color on the planet which would eventually mutate itself out into one color. Then there would not be any races.

So, the question is what was the **original DNA** that we all started from on the tree of life DNA? How did it become changed through the process of having different colors, different features, different capabilities and all these other factions that take place in reproducing because of different DNA? Here again if it is not a research type of project that we are dealing with, then what other hidden reason could you come up with for all these individuals to create all these things? Things that you would not know or take for granted. Remember that it would lead to a product that is out of your realm of thinking that everybody has to be wrong because you have not thought of that before.

What is **universe all DNA**? You have to understand that universe all DNA starts even with the Egyptians changing the DNA to try to transform different heads on different people. This is what we call transferring the DNA around and trying to transmix people and to make hybrids, chameleons and all these other types of things.

The Universe All DNA actually started when we first saw the relief pictures of the Egyptian pyramids with these different looking animals on the side of them. That is how long they have been trying to do this universe all DNA to show us that they can create the composite chameleon monsters that we are not used to seeing and having around us. They are looking for the universe all DNA. Instead of cutting the head off of something to put it on another body with the DNA already established they are trying to do it with the universe all DNA to create DNA that can form to fit the individual's desire and needs. Not just gender but everything else that we talk about such as eyes, facial features, hair, skin color, height, and weight.

The Wall of Humanity at Puma Punku in Bolivia has over forty carved stone heads of various races or species of all of the different types of extraterrestrials that have been here and probably shared their DNA. The stone figureheads are there to represent the extraterrestrials' science of their DNA to show that they created all these different species through the DNA that they manufactured. So how many people actually colonized the Earth? According to the number of figureheads it is forty representing all of the different types of extraterrestrials that have been here and probably shared their DNA. Which is probably the people that we have here on our planet now that we have around us. That is another way to look at it.

What I am saying is that the figureheads were a facsimile of the different types of DNA that were originally set up on our planet to repopulate and stimulate a new type of humans that would lay and breed together. Therefore, out of the mix of all these different types of DNA that they had on the figureheads from Puma Punku is that very possibly as we all lay together and interbreed together we will come up with the Earth's dominant DNA.

Why did they have all these figureheads there for us to see yet no explanation for them? I am saying this is a way for these figureheads to show all the other extraterrestrials that the planet is going through a process of deducing all these types of DNA down to the original **dominant DNA** of our planet for several reasons. If you do the medical examination of trying to crack the DNA code for whatever reason to find out if it was a special DNA code. Anyway, it is a possibility to make a mutant DNA code out of it but the whole point of what we are trying to say here with the study of the DNA and the figureheads is that very possibly the reducing or deducing of all these figureheads I guess that they put there eventually to recreate another type of civilization. I believe that all the figureheads at Puma Punku are the re-creation of civilization lost or the realization of a new civilization that they can try to do more DNA experiments trying to find out how to make a new DNA. Why were the figureheads on the wall at Puma Punku? They had to be put there for a reason to represent something.

What we are going to say here before we forget it is that with the universe all DNA imagine when Jesus Christ and all of those people were put on planet Earth that they represented the white faction of Jesus Christ and God. Then you go ahead and you have the forty different figureheads on the stone wall at Puma Punku, right? The figureheads represent in my opinion the DNA that the extraterrestrials had that were here before in the past. This was the start for them to be remembered. The only realization I can come up with of why you have all these individuals featured there is that they represented their own type of DNA from wherever they came from or whatever planet they came from. They were placed here at the same time as God and Christ who represented the whites and all the other factions represented all the colors of the DNA that they did.

So therefore, the search for more universe all DNA exists. And there again they start all over again and that could be very much where we are right now. It is going to the same process of a planetary mix of all of our DNA to come up with the universe all DNA for what reason? And the reason is this, the transformation from being an animal or whatever it is on the planet to try to transform yourself into a living walking human being and yet maintaining to keep your consciousness and your experiences with you. That is the question of universe all DNA, it is to find out if there is a way that we can do this to make it all possible.

I guess another way to look at this weeding process of the DNA is that it may be possible the extraterrestrials went through the same process of actually weeding out who they might turn out to be. We do not know the end result but we are just trying to come up with the understanding of the process here. The extraterrestrials and the society where they came from may have done the same thing that we were going through on this planet as far as laying together and breeding together and making a universal being for that planet at that time as their evolutionary state of human beings on it.

A very good possibility of why the extraterrestrials are around is the question of their DNA. What if it is the possibility that they are trying to figure out what happened to their DNA which enabled them to be able to reproduce? Or maybe their DNA became stagnant and just created drones through the process of research in their science labs? Here again when they went through the mixing of colors it ended up with we do not know how many or who they started with the configuration. We are not privy to that. Maybe they are trying to find out what happened to their original DNA. Or maybe as we study our DNA they can see and repair theirs. What other reason would they be studying our DNA if not to repair theirs or improve theirs or make it better somehow or to change the DNA structure.

You have a commingling of DNA to do what? In my point of view, it is to come up with the mathematical solution to the universe all DNA. To be able to take an alien and be able to change their DNA so they can appear more in society and get along with us.

We know that the DNA has to change because of all of the different noses and faces and sizes of all the forty different stone figureheads that were on the wall at Puma Punku. So, with all these different figureheads and the mathematical probability, how do you change the DNA on your noses, your lips, your ears, your faces, your hands, your arms, and other parts? This actually could be a science test that if the inhabitants could not go ahead and achieve the goal and figure out how to do the mathematical problem of how to splice or mutate or change the DNA that they do not graduate. So, in other words, it is like the DNA structure and science of it all is nothing more than a mathematical problem of the different features of the human body.

And now also that universe all DNA is being spoken and thought of, wouldn't it be neat if universe all DNA was a way of grafting and filling in the gaps between the DNA so the individuals that were created would be tolerable to look at and therefore associate with? This has to be the transference of the individual trying to become a human and not having the perfect DNA as we have it. Think of it this way, if you were the extraterrestrials and you were not pleasant to look at and you scared everybody on the planet would you not want to change yourself so you would not startle everyone around you? Of course you would. So, if you do not want to startle and scare others then you would come up with a universe all DNA that would allow you a choice of the seven to ten different noses and lips combinations. So, imagine trying to fill in those gaps and create a human that basically has the proper DNA to look right and be acceptable. This is what all this is. Universe all DNA is a grafting kind of positioning of stuff to allow other human forms of this nature.

There is a universe all DNA hunt that goes on maybe so we can take these entities from a reptile or a bird or any other type of animal on earth to understand how many times they are going to live, die, and repeat to try to transfer into being a human. The universe all DNA quest is to make this situation a faster process for these individuals instead of going through hundreds and hundreds of years to be able to slowly evolve like the Darwin type of evolution. Universe all DNA is a sped up version of a mathematical process that forms to fill in the desired specifications of the mechanic building it. It is nothing more than that.

Universe all DNA is the **creative DNA** that will allow them to modify the DNA. It is nothing but a math problem to be able to make grafting tissue into large areas to cover up improper DNA matches such as if you are a reptilian form and you are trying to become transferred into becoming a human through the change of the DNA in a slow process through birth and rebirth. That is why we have this thing called reincarnation. So actually, to me the study of universe all DNA is to have a universal DNA that would allow all of these different functions to be adjusted.   And it is the **adjustable universe all DNA** that they can adjust to fit gaps in your physical makeup. They are probably now trying to hurry up this DNA changing process in a shorter amount of time instead of living a long period of time to get to the step of the universe all DNA. In other words, instead of it having to live, die, be reborn a thousand times, it is to be able to do it in one time with the universe all DNA.

So, what the extraterrestrials were saying to us is that they do not know how to create a universe all bonding type of DNA which would cover more of this or that or whatever the dysfunction may be at the time. Imagine if you are one of these reptiles or something that is trying to become a human and you have a way of trying to speed up the grafting process to make it where it is a universe all DNA. It is a **manipulative universe all DNA** that can reach and span in the areas that they want to make it easier for them to be accepted in human society. Before universe all DNA it is very likely impossible for the grafting of such things.

The universe all DNA is a quest for being able to take any form of life and transfer it into a walking about human being. If you were that animal and you wanted to become a human being think of all the times to have to live, die, be reborn for a normal process of the DNA to transfer and grow into a human being. All this is a search for a faster way to make a universe all DNA that is pliable and flexible to figure out how to do the math to create such DNA. If you are trying to change the DNA according to Darwin's point of evolution look at how long it took. My point of universe all DNA is a faster process that would allow it to take place.

We are possibly the **stimulus DNA** which means that the extraterrestrials or aliens that are here are really a product end result from either their previous planet of laying together and producing this type of individual and this is their DNA. The individuals from all these other different planets might be a result of their DNA research project that either went wrong or sterile. We do not really know the reason why but we know this is a study for the DNA that has never been seen before on our planet. This DNA that we have been looking for universally allows us to change and configure our DNA from a reptile to a human being through time and processing of not only of evolution but through the grafting of DNA from one form to how many times it would take. That is what universe all DNA is.

We are saying that we are a science experiment. They can change our DNA global wide by just impregnating all these other people with different types of DNA that came from the extraterrestrials to best make the melting pot. This deduces down to these outstanding facial features to show that the DNA is being assembled on the faces of the people that are walking on the planet now. This leads you to believe that this is a science research project which says all DNA is a mathematical process that they are changing from what we were into what they want us to look like. It also shows you that there is a medical research possibility going on to be able to manipulate DNA changes. What could be the reason for that? The reason is to learn how to transform DNA in something such as a reptile into a human being through the process.

Are the glial cells in our brain a DNA possibility that the extraterrestrials have actually entered into us to put the glial in us so we can activate and open up our mind and our speech and therefore cause us to evolve even at a faster rate? You just have so many different variables. It is all controlled in this one human standard clone of the body that has all these Play Dough™ or Mr. Potato Head™ like things that you can add or take off of it. Why don't you understand it is just a science project and the only way to graduate is to solve the problem? That would be great. It is a never ending subject.

What is the point of universe all DNA? Are we trying to create a mind that is a better thinker? Is it basically to get everybody together to try to allow the mind to produce at one hundred percent efficiency? Is that what it is all about? Or is it to stimulate the glial cells so we can develop other regions of the mind that have not been developed already? Is that not another study to allow the glial cells to grow in our mind so we can become smarter and greater?

I am not really that educated on this kind of subject. I am just an observer. Anyway, ask yourself why your noses are not bigger or your teeth different or your ears larger? What makes it, what makes yourself you? In other words what DNA did your parents have when they shared together that one over dominated the other? At what point does this all start? Does this start with the heat of the egg at conception? That is a very logical point of view because supposedly if the egg is not hot enough it goes to female. If it is not cold enough it goes to male or whichever the reverse is. I am not sure of that. But here again it is nothing more than a science experiment of how to either guarantee the male or female specie by the temperature of the fertile eggs in her womb such as we do with all the other animals in the world. Why can we not do it ourselves? So the whole idea is to understand what made you have the nose that you have, have the ears that you have, have all these forms instead of the ones from the other parent that you did not inherit these features from. Do you understand what I am saying? So here again it makes you wonder if they want someone to be a piano player why they did not make somebody with longer fingers.

We assume that there has to be another physical form for this DNA to exist so we could cohabitate. In reality they just change our DNA or insert this other form of mathematical DNA which has another protein or amino acid or whatever it has in it to cause its dominance or whatever for the child to grow with their DNA gene in it. At what point does what gene at what thing do to start the avalanche? I think at conception basically starts the perception of the being itself but then as it evolves when does the sexuality take place? When do all of the other features in the body know it is going to be female versus male? The question I am asking is it at conception or is it after the basic gene of the basic human is formed and then they go ahead and they have A, B, and C done and now we need to do D, E, and F and finish the situation? It is just a point of paying attention.

But then you have all the inter-seeding and intermixing and interchanging of the DNA. How can you have intermixing and all this other DNA without sexual reproduction? The only way that can happen is if you are doing a science experiment and know how to interject it into the normal or the clone DNA to cause it to have a change. You follow? The same thing is what we need to do with our periodic table of elements to add different things that we have here on the planet to make new and better.

The reason we might be going through this mixing nature of the DNA around the planet could be for a more renounced reason in that the refugees from these planets that came here are trying to reestablish their DNA of what they look like from their planet through more and more numbers so there can be more of them in a quicker form of reproducing. Therefore that could also be possibly another reason for the planet Earth here being turned into a gene pool of mixing together to try to reestablish the original gene pool that they had from the forty figureheads that are on our planet at Puma Punku now to repopulate and to recreate the people that were on the asteroid planet themselves.

Remember everything that we are talking about and everything that we are doing on this planet has already been produced and has been done before. We are only a rediscovery of all these things. We made nothing new originally. Nothing. We are just participants. We are like the tea color in water. Basically, we are all just waiting to see what comes out.

CHAPTER FOUR

UNIVERSE ALL DNA

The Science Research Project

What did the extraterrestrials change to make us into their image? Did they give us speech or what? Then could you maybe understand that there may be a larger picture which was for these individuals to have come to our own Earth to change us into their own image. That was the original sin and mistake that made them to have become trapped here on the planet Earth. They cannot go home because of the sin that they have done. Without the extraterrestrials changing and tainting us we have no idea of what we would have been.

I guess that another way to look at this weeding process of the DNA is that it may be possible that the extraterrestrials went through the same process here. In other words what I am trying to say is that the extraterrestrials and the society where they came from may have done the same thing that we are going through on this planet as far as laying together and breeding together and making a universal being for that planet. At the end of that mutation stuff, what are the dominant colors and features of the dominant DNA of that planet at that time as their evolutionary state of human beings on it?

A very good possibility of why the extraterrestrials are around and all is the question of their DNA. What if it is the possibility of they are trying to figure out what happened to their DNA which enables them to be able to reproduce or make their DNA to become stagnant and just create drones through the process of their science research labs?

So why are the extraterrestrials not looking for where they came from? Remember if they did not create the DNA they are having to study it as a science research project. If they were not good enough to create the original DNA themselves then the secret of DNA is still hidden from them and they do not know how to do the mathematical problem. This certifies my ideas for the reason for the DNA structure to have taken place. If they already had the answer to how to do it then they would not be asking us the question and putting us through the torture and torment and most important of all wasting their time waiting for the gene pool to exist to create the genes that they have for their research test on the finished product. They have to wait for the period of time for the essence of everything to produce this

DNA so they can test it to see if they can find the hidden gateway that they are looking for to allow them to be able to change the DNA.

What if the extraterrestrials were trying to change our shape and form to become exactly what they are through more DNA manipulation? Now this could also lead into the point of view of the swirling and the laying together and producing all the different colors in the world to try to find the agenda that they are trying to achieve. Think of it from the other side that the extraterrestrials are trying to make us look more like them or they look more like us. Also, what if the extraterrestrials were having unknown sex with these individual women that they took up with them in their spaceships? And the extraterrestrials slowly administer their DNA to the children that they produced with these Earth women. Then they start to form it into the society of the world where we live. So, I am wondering how many DNAs the extraterrestrials may have sub-seeded into our civilization and our people here to go ahead and make their own selves become the dominant species on the planet. We are never going to know all of the answers. We are just going to have to keep an open mind until we come to the answer.

This universe all DNA could now be that the extraterrestrials are now being known to exist and that possibly more of their inhabitants have been taken away or abducted and then they came back to have children. The children that were taken from them after they laid together could have been a way of inserting the extraterrestrials' DNA again and again more and more into what we look like to change us into what they look like. All you have to do is look at the nose, the mouth, and all these other things to see if you think you are capable of seeing how it represents the extraterrestrials that I have seen so far. Look at the mouth, the thinning of the nose, and the area under the nose and above the upper lip.

One thing that I believe that they are doing is putting one DNA change in each of these people that they share their sex and evolution with so that one person will go out and share the DNA. Now this does not mean that they have not done the same thing to five hundred or five thousand people with the same results to influence it better. I believe that is what the extraterrestrials were doing with the captive women that they took from planet Earth. Then these women and their children were brought back and the children are now left on the planet to start introducing more alien DNA and making us all look like the same thing. Is this a mixing of the pot of the DNA to make it inside the same way? To make a clone type or a magnification type of limited evidence instead of having individuality with different facial features to the point of dissolving the old style human beings to make a more streamlined and new model for some reason. It could be a way of getting rid of the undesirable

DNA to bring forth the new product of the new human DNA thing.

I wonder what other DNA the extraterrestrials are seeding into us that might make us look more like Egyptians or more of this or that. Remember from the over forty stone figureheads that were on the wall at Puma Punku that all those different DNA configurations that are on this planet here in a spiraling situation to commingle and lay together to maybe produce a one world color point of view on the planet with the inhabitants. Therefore, it would be a one world color and a one world DNA because if you do not have any variances in your DNA and everything then it goes back to being everything in the same pool. Then wait a minute, if you do not have any fresh DNA that makes it impossible to create all this other stuff. So, it might be nothing more than just a way to put us into their DNA gene pool to extrapolate what they want from us and be able to throw us back out into the field of science over again. I would say it is a science research thing.

Maybe we are here as a gene pool for all the different extraterrestrials on the planet Earth so they can commingle us all together and pick the DNA that they want to take with them. Then they can better introduce this fresh new DNA and run it through the process of the Earth's women and laying together and doing the situation. This might be another way for the extraterrestrials to have used us on planet Earth as a magical

DNA that was sent off into the world that they never knew existed to basically bring their gene pool back up to full status as they were in the beginning. In other words, we might be lost in a DNA gene pool that they need to bring back home so they can make themselves one hundred percent of what they originally used to be.

Think of all those different figureheads here on planet Earth, okay, as a gene pool and now that we are all going to be mixed together and will eventually become a one gene pool that becomes a drone, a norm, the consistency of the same color and all. What will the nose or the ears of this person look like? All I am asking here is will it deduce us down to the possibility of us looking like the extraterrestrials as their next situation?

What really gets me going here is the extraterrestrials coming down here with all their people and laying it on the planet Earth like they have done. So actually they are waiting for all the different laying together and breeding together to develop and take place in order to see the color that manifests then. I do not know what the kind of person would look like, a white person maybe, or whatever the case may be. But that might be what they are trying to do. They may be coming out with a new fresh dominant one hundred percent DNA individual that has a fresh new blood with however many years of reproductive cycle that they want to go through it. The real end game here is all about reproduction and getting fresh DNA as it possibly is. Remember you always have to get new fresh blood somewhere so it only makes sense of billions of years of space.

It just strikes me positively that I have discovered a magical new point of view that all of the other alien civilizations donated their DNA of the best person that they had as a better representation from their planet to our planet here and seeded us all at the same time, the same area, and the same place. That might have been a primitive manner or not. But whatever manner they were seeded let's say that they already had the reproductive capabilities and maybe the abilities to speak and could do all that because all the ones that are down here on this planet if you really examine the DNA have the ability to speak.

Now if they changed our DNA on our planet only and we only came here as a favorite of God and Christ then that only changed the DNA of the strains of the people here. They came here and changed all the DNA here, all the different strains, and here the only way for you to do that is commingling together to produce the final fruit of all the situations of laying together. Maybe possibly this could be the achieving goal of the extraterrestrials. Why would you not share your DNA with these people?

Maybe their DNA became diseased or whatever the case may be. They could not bring themselves out of having this DNA difficulty and that is why they needed fresh DNA to get themselves out of this DNA situation. Basically, I believe what was happening on all the individual planets that seeded our planet here with their DNA was that they were going dormant. There was no change and they became the clone on each planet that I had talked about with the laying together and reproducing their image on the planet and then coming here and hopefully trying to lay the different images together to see what in the world they would produce and what the outcome would be. And maybe the laying together of all these individuals might naturally give us the one hundred percent efficiency that we need to open up and have the ability to retain and gain one hundred percent uses of our mind.

The whole point about the extraterrestrials' DNA and how they are seeding us and doing it all is that no matter what you go through, the dedications in your life, the hardships that you deal with, it eventually is preparing you for the end game in which you are going to have to prepare. Unfortunately, the end game that you cannot get rid of is called death.

So here again the point of view of this is that you just have to keep your eyes open to see and understand the telltale signs that are on the television screen in front of you. When you watch the different people on the television over and over again and again you eventually start seeing the differences where one side of a person's mouth or face of how the DNA did not really make a really good fit. But here again it shows you obviously all

DNA does not mix perfectly together. When it does not mix perfectly together like it is supposed to do then we have these hybrids and stuff that were created through intermixing. Then you have research institutes and hospitals which study and try to understand what happened to the DNA and what happened to the bonding between two cells and energy.

Maybe that is another thing they are trying to find out about in this structure of understanding through everything. Maybe just the unholiness that they might release with their knowing everything about the DNA. So if you slow yourself down and admit to yourself that there could be these other planets out there would you not think that all these planets would not have a full medical base trying to figure out the problems that they created in their society of people that are breeding together to stop any kind of mutation in their desire or anything. So evidently here again you have to realize you never know the unknown DNA out there that they have not ever commingled with laying together. So, what we are asking ourselves and having to admit and having to realize that this was probably going on in a thousand or a million or however many different planets all the time.

So, the question is where did they go to until they come back? They do not come back until the mixing of DNA is complete and all of their science research projects are done. They do not come back until all of the other people here assimilate all of the information and knowledge that we had done to think we are in charge so they can take information from us. Isn't that the desire of all science projects? To be able to take the cream off the top and the best of all that has been done. It sort of makes sense that all of a sudden that these diseased planets are not even capable of wildlife. See, we do not understand what they did to the DNA and how it might have affected everything on their planet. Can you imagine that? Then they come here to planet Earth as if we are a go-to store of life which we are and take whatever birds, reptiles, wildlife, whatever it is that we have and take them back as they need to start the evolutionary planet over again if that is so the case. So, the research project was to make and revive their planet. Then the point of view is to make it happen quicker and faster.

So here again, if you think about it from a better point of projection is that the extraterrestrials are taking what we have already on the planet Earth as a living viable creature, a fish, whatever in the oceans, or whatever you want to think and they take those with them back to their planet. Think about how fast it would already seed the planet ahead of time if you already had good working viable reptiles and stuff to represent the direction in which the humans were going instead of taking a billion years. Instead you cut it in half and then again the next time we go through the same process of the one-fourth of a billion years for so on and so forth.

It makes you think back and wonder are we not here for a reason. We are here basically if we are a residue of them to show to everybody else and all the DNA out there that they are commingling together to have a purpose, to have a reasoning, to have a force, to have an unveiling, and to have a bit of information to share with everybody that only we were able to gather together to be sure.

It makes you wonder about the Egyptians' DNA and where did they really come from originally. I do not think that the Egyptians are one of the forty different displays of figureheads at Puma Punku. But here again if you do not have the Egyptians on this wall it would lead you to believe that the Egyptians might have been the first ones here. Because all the figureheads at Puma Punku were exactly those people that the DNA infected this planet to do some kind of research project. So the research project was to make and revive their planet and all the other things. Anyway, we do not know. We are just guessing as to what is on the wall of figureheads at Puma Punku.

What I am trying to say about the Egyptians is that their faces seem to be mathematically perfect when we look at them. Nobody has facial features that are mathematically perfect that I can see as far as one side is this way and one side is that way. So in the figure that is carved in marble or stone in the area that represents the Egyptians how could it be mathematically perfect if it was carved by hand? Therefore, this tells you it could not have been carved by hand but was carved by machine doing perfection work. This perfect representation of the physical faces had to have been mechanically done by the extraterrestrials.

What I guess they keep trying to do with our DNA is to have a **perfection DNA** which is perfect for their ability to be able to take it apart and house it and create it like they want to do. It is called perfection DNA that they have been trying to do for billions of years and now we just realized that they are trying to cut down this time into a shorter amount of time of however many years it take to rehash it to get quicker and faster results.

So, then you could have the growth so they could start this DNA project through the weeding process of trying to get a pure DNA or the **ultimate DNA.** So, as you and I understand that then the only time the extraterrestrials are going to show up is when the DNA mixing is complete. It is close to that time when their DNA mixing is complete and maybe when we are all one color. They come back and reapply the planet with the complete DNA that they got and the end result with everybody mixing together is we are all one color. Now does that make sense to you? So now that we realize that it is getting close to the DNA mixing time to come together that the whole point of it would be to make the planet become or go through the good versus evil thing as mentioned in the Bible about Armageddon.

This is just another way of purifying the planet. Instead of purifying just the planet maybe before on the asteroid belt planet they might have purified the DNA a little bit too much or did not have their math together or whatever and the planet exploded. Maybe that is what happened to the asteroid belt as another way to be able to understand and realize how the planet exploded with some logical reason that makes sense to us as we are trying to bring forth to do. Now that the spaceships are being shown on the television news programs you have to understand how far it projects me to go to the next step even further out there in the imagination.

Now unfortunately if they used their war to purify their planet could this not kill all the whole bunch of other DNA and then allow the rest of the people that lay together to become the final group of DNA people that lay together? That would basically be the reducing down of the people on the planet to finally end up with a one color world, one race, one being clone normally on the planet. Is that not the full cycle of the planet as has been brought today to realize for the first time ever as far as I know?

The reason the extraterrestrials are trapped here is because they are the ones that changed our DNA here originally and started the reform or change on the planet before it was originally decided to do. Maybe that is why they had to originally decide to have to come here is because they had exploded the fifth planet that we call the asteroid belt and destroyed Mars so bad that it was uninhabitable and they had to come here. Yes, that is the facts because there is evidence of the nuclear destruction there by the residue left on the surface of Mars. Now we do not know who lived on the asteroid belt planet but we will one day be able to figure it out. Maybe that is what we are doing on this planet now. We are taking the remnants of the people that were alive from that point of view from that planet and bringing them here to this planet and trying to repopulate and remake their civilization that they destroyed on their planet however many billions of years ago.

Remember that there is a **dominant DNA** that you have not heard about. I believe what we are trying to do is find a dominant DNA chain that might have started the earth. Dominant DNA is the DNA that basically over ran or conquered the other person that you had sex with. In other words, when you have a mother and a father and they have a child and the child has different attributes from each one. Why did they take the mother's attributes instead of the father's attributes? Why did the nose come from the mother's genes and the mouth come from the father's genes? What makes the child choose which DNA dominates from which parent and therefore hacking back and forth in time? It is called the dominant DNA.

So, what makes one gene more dominant over another gene? It is probably an amino acid or something of this nature that outlasts the other one or conquers the other one. I am not really educated on this topic. But something mathematically over powered or overcame it in order to exist and live in the world. If you can figure out if this DNA was inner bred or mixed out of the unit to find out what the hidden DNA was. What DNA linked them together to create a base?

DNA is a mathematical problem that has been set out through everything to make it possible and that is why dominant DNA is important to understand. If there is a dominant DNA in all of the millions of people that laid together and made this possible, what would the extraterrestrials be looking for with all of these different people? It is almost as if they are looking for the dominant DNA. Can you imagine if we could finally deduce what the original dominant DNA was originally? To be able to put a picture on a person to basically see what a dominant DNA person would look like with all his attributes before it was reamed out. In other words, is any individual one hundred percent anything?

Dominant DNA is what rules and conquers and makes you have the facial features and attributes that you have. But here again, you have to remember the extraterrestrial or ancient alien type of deal of the universe all DNA. Universe all DNA is what the extraterrestrials are looking for when we are being laid together to come up with this different type of protein or acid or whatever it is. It is the universe all DNA that they use when they transfer a reptile or some kind of mammal into a human being basically to transcend them from the animal that they were into a mind or progressionary step of science into a human being. In other words the universe all DNA is the DNA that allows us to create more features to become a human being. Universe all DNA is a worldwide search to find a way to be able to take any body or any shape or any size, any mammal anywhere and be able to transfer them into being a walking breathing human being.

Just imagine that you are a scientist trying to help someone in the burn unit of the hospital to have something that would grow new skin instead of grafting skin from another part of the body in order to change the person. With dominant DNA they are trying to mathematically make skin and flesh to cover up those areas. We are just a science project and we do not even know it because the wool is pulled over our eyes. When you have dominant DNA whether it is a big nose or a smooth area above the lips, they are trying to figure out how to do the math. You can only look at the unfortunate situation that happens to children born with birth defects. This is the improper mixing of the normal DNA and so we are trying to find out why it did not mix or what went wrong or why it did happen.

If you really just think about it, all of the twisting and the coming together as we are going to do while we are here is that all these different species here on earth could not have come from just Adam and Eve. They came from somebody else so that all these other people were put here in a gene pool. Okay, so is the gene pool here a site for the most dominant of DNA that this DNA represents or whatever the individual or discipline of the DNA is? And so the basic idea is that eventually all the people that are laying together on the planet Earth will end up deducing and reducing themselves and reproducing themselves down into what we would call a dominant DNA of the planet. This is because they have run all of the others off as we have been interbreeding and interbreeding.

There again with the dominant DNA you also have the one skin color or one world color. So, ask yourself the point of view, is the reasoning of what they are doing is to deduce it down so they can get to what the real final color is? Is that what the real final dominant DNA is, or are they doing this so maybe it is just a science fiction thing here? So, if you mix everything down to one color to one of this and one of that, what is your answer? What would you say the reasoning is for all this to happen over all these thousands of years to come to this conclusion? It is just the way things happen. Evidently you are not a mathematician or whatever if you do not understand how much time it takes to do all these things.

The chance of the DNA there to go ahead and see if they couldn't reproduce the people from the past is that possibly in the past when they were doing their science project of DNA is that they got to the point of the dominant DNA where the DNA couldn't reproduce or become anything else or became sterile and would not activate. They are hoping to stop the sterilization of the human species. In other words, the dominant DNA ends up being the dominant DNA and at what point does the dominant DNA not become acceptable to make and continue life on. What I am saying is that the human being DNA is the same as a plant type of stuff was like ten to twelve different times before the seed itself rejuvenates and possibly becomes sterile and cannot produce. That is what very possibly happened to them when they tried this DNA experiment on us. It backfired on them and destroyed everything because when you thin and keep thinning something out you break through the wall and let the floodgates open that you had held closed. Therefore, we do not know if it was a disease at this time which ran rampantly over the face of the earth or was it something else that they had been trying to contain all this time. It is just a matter of understanding.

Let us see what these dominant DNA genes produce after all these extraterrestrials come to this planet for a science project. Which of these hundreds of different human beings existed that could have been the dominant DNA chain on this planet? There again maybe they are still trying to find their dominant DNA. What purpose does dominant DNA do? I do not know the answer. If you know the answer, let me know.

Why do we have **left over DNA** that we do not seem to use or do the scientists call it left over DNA because we do not use it? What else could this DNA be used for? You have heard them say that our gene pool has been changed a lot. The key thing that you have to listen to is that you have other DNAs in your existing pool that they do not know what they are there for. So we have inactive DNA. It is not activated but you are still carrying it with you. So, if it ever was to be activated it would be there.

So, it sounds like to me that we are carrying a host of different possibilities of what we could be. Now we can either transcend into being more than the human being that we are with this or we can go the other way. So, if you have extra DNA in you, what if this extra DNA is left over DNA? Okay, is the extra DNA in your body left over from another period in time when you used to be some other type of animal like a snake, a reptile, a bird, a dog, or something of this nature? Or just reverse it one hundred eighty degrees. This DNA could be there to be activated so you can be turned into a dog or cat or whatever the case may be.

Okay, so what would you think the other uses would be for this extra DNA in you? I am trying to perceive it to be a positive one way and yet positive the other way. So, if it is DNA that has not been used yet, then explain why the aliens had to attach on to us something to give us speech. What did they change in our DNA? If the aliens or the extraterrestrials can change the DNA, then what is it you don't understand? We are all scientific lab rats with the genetic base and they are taking us from one way to the other depending on how we turn out. It is a science lab experiment. It is all that we are. I know that it is hard to accept that you actually are a science experiment and they are doing your DNA algorithms.

There is **unknown DNA** and you don't know what it is, however the logic doesn't mean you don't know what it is there for. It means we are not educated enough to ask correct questions. So, is that what this DNA would be used for, what it leads to, what it is? Does it lead to having extra limbs? Does it lead to a different tail? Does it lead to feathers? What is this DNA that is left over? Do we have the science to tell us what it does? Do you know if it is inactive DNA? Okay, it is inactive DNA which you carry it with you. It sounds like to me that we are just a rolling chassis of DNA running down the street and they are going to change us and develop us into whatever they want, whenever they want, and we will not ever know the difference. Actually the question is, how would you ever know? You would not, would you, especially if they control your algorithms and everything.

The point of universe all DNA is how can you use DNA? What other uses would DNA be for? It is apparent that we could have been animals that live in the past or birds in the future if you just change your DNA, right? So why did they change our DNA for this point now? Why are there so many humans on the planet instead of so many birds and everything? Why is the dominant specie our way of looking at it of more and more humans and more and more times?

What I am saying is they are looking for a missing DNA, a secret DNA, a universe all DNA, a perfect DNA, an adjustable DNA, a programmable DNA. What happened to the DNA from the people who lived for hundreds of years? Where did the DNA go from Enoch and Methuselah? And just how maybe they are trying to recreate that same DNA on Earth as an excuse or search for the fountain of youth? Most like all of these people are gone and what a task to try and recreate this point of the fountain of youth DNA. So if you have **programmable DNA**, then the only thing they could be doing with us is trying to develop more DNA for a topic that we do not know.

I have been talking about trying to find out where the mutation takes place in the difference of the DNA, of when it activates and causes a wider nose or a lip or the eyes or whatever they are possibly looking for in that type of DNA. And then is that DNA the dominant DNA on the planet? Has this been done before on another planet and that is why the extraterrestrials are the way they are, trying to regroup, reform, make a civilization of this from only a few individuals that escaped the planet Earth? It makes sense if you just take the science fiction out of it.

What is the reason for all of us laying together to

produce one colored individuals that are the dominant DNA or the not dominant DNA? What we are looking for is called **programmable DNA** which covers all the different colors. Programmable DNA is what I am trying to figure out how to do the math on. Then there is medical DNA where they go in and medically change your DNA for this frozen procedure that we are doing now such as for Alzheimer's and things of that nature.

Our DNA is the master chemistry set. We do not even know how and what we can produce with all the different types of formulas and stuff that we have. It is like the Yin and Yang brothers on the planet Earth being able to experiment with all the different types of humans to see what they come out with as an end form game. We have discussed this before. The end form game would cycle back to the original DNA which would be one color and one way of thinking. Usually that is the case if it does not stop its own self out. Eventually out of the weeding out of all the stuff comes the ultra DNA, the refining of all the others. In other words, you come back to the original creation of the DNA very possibly.

I guess what they are trying to find out is how to create DNA. Nobody has had the ability to create it. They can graft it and do this and do that but they have not been able to create it. Most likely that is the hidden trick, I guess. Now that would be the question? What form did the original DNA have as a facial recognition? What form was a face before there was a face?

How did they know to make a face? Does the face represent a face? Here again lies the rub of the scalp, the itch, the feel with the satisfaction of the scratch. What did they use for a mold or a beginning to know what a face is supposed to look like? See here again guys you have to realize somebody had to create a face. It is the greatest and the most never ending asking question it ever is. How did we ever become where we are to look like we are?

Who just started or who ever created DNA? Really, I mean is it like the greatest chemistry set they ever got? Well of course it is. Look at the products you get to make and these products learn how to reproduce and make more products. Only my God, it is either we have an invasive weed on the face of the earth which is most likely, or we have something that can really become educated. There are so many of us here they have got to be extrapolating information from us because it seems to be what we have the most of.

I always seem to come back to the point of view that they are always trying to find out how to either create original DNA or extend it or reclaim something that has been lost. I guess you would say from the beginning to the end is what I have tried to discover about the DNA. The only thing that comes logical to my way of having positive thinking is that they want to regain and figure out how they can reestablish the original DNA that allowed us to live for thousands of years or thousand years long. Our life expectancy is becoming shorter because we do not know how to keep our insides alive and fresher than they were when we were let us say twenty years old. If we could keep our organs and everything in the condition that they were in a younger stage of our age, then we could live for a whole lot longer. When we eat the wrong foods or do the wrong kind of things here that causes our own demise because we remove the essence that keeps us youthful. When you think of yourself as a battery but you do not take care of it then battery eventually goes dead. The same is true for you because the worse you treat it then the faster it dies. It is just a matter of realization factors. If you do not drink pure water, then how are you going to be able to clean anything out of your system. If you do not consume pure stuff, then you are contaminating yourself. Just think how bad that is. Anyway, it is a complete circle. DNA is what they are trying to find out.

A summation or an answer to all of the questions. We are all just a science project. You have to realize and understand the Darwin theory of evolution and you just have to understand what we would have become if we would not have been changed by the UFOs and the extraterrestrials. The extraterrestrials who changed our DNA stole our planet so they could take it over. That was the original sin, changing our DNA. The extraterrestrials that came here stole our planet and changed us from what we would have become to what we are now. They are the ones who changed our DNA and made us what we are now.

CHAPTER FIVE

THE SUN

The Mother of the Planets

The abundant sun that we take for granted. The giver of light and heat and energy. How did it get there? Why is it there? What fuel does it use? How long will it last? How can we keep the sun alive longer so it does not go supernova and destroys everything? If the sun does go supernova will it destroy all the planets that it has created and therefore creating a vacuum in space because the solar system has been used to the point of extinction? If that happens will they start all over with another new sun that they created and put together with the natural resources that they have assembled someplace?

Let's start at the beginning with how the sun was created. Scientists theorize that the sun was formed from a giant, rotating cloud of gas and dust known as the solar nebula. Gravity drew this gas and dust together to create the sun. The gas and dust clumped together to form a protostar that eventually became the sun.

In the Bible in the first chapter of the book of Genesis it says that God created the Heaven and the Earth and darkness was upon the face of the deep. And God said, "let there be light" and there was light. God said for the light to divide the day from the night and to be a sign and to be for the days, and the seasons, and years. God set the light in the heaven to give light upon the earth. This light is the sun.

I believe that the extraterrestrials created the sun to produce the planets. The sun is the mother of the planets. The sun to me is the mother that birthed all the planets. Therefore, I am going to the next step and connecting the dots to say that the planets are actually the eggs that allowed everything and the birth to be done from them. As well as you could consider the egg to be the sun itself and therefore these are the children from within it. Is God the sun? Is Mother Nature the sun? Is Father Nature the sun and everything that it creates? The question I have is who created the sun? Where did the sun come from? That is too much to bite off from this point of view. I guess I will have to come and take myself to the extraterrestrial library so I can understand it.

The sun could be called a birth canal. Now think about that. It is a birthing canal for the planets. The planets had to be birthed through a birthing canal or some area and remember the good shot could also be what we call the birthing canal or being pushed out of it. It is just one of those types of things you ponder about. You will never know the proper terminology unless you keep trying.

It is just hard to realize or be able to understand that the sun itself is like a mother guarding her children. It was created to get hot to produce and create the planets which were eventually put in orbit out there and later to be harvested by people coming by and mining from them whatever they thought they needed from that planet. It is just hard to basically realize that we are nothing more than a mining solar system that has extraterrestrials that know how to do this process a whole lot better than we do.

Ask yourself logically where else could the planets have come from. Look at the large size of the sun and small size of the planets and you are asking me how else could they have got there if they were not birthed from the sun? I wonder what they would call this process in extraterrestrial terminology.

The sun is the largest essence creator. In other words, it deduces down to make the essence and then it spits it out creating the planets. Every sun does the same thing to create a solar system in another part of space. I keep hitting around it but the sun is the essence of all of our life. It is the essence and the creator and maker. It makes you wonder where did the essence all come from that the extraterrestrials put in a huge large electronical sphere that they created.

No matter how many times we talk about the sun, you have to realize that it all deduces back to where did the original essence come from? Where did the essence come from that they would have even put inside the creation that we call the sun? Then activate the essence in the sun so it would produce the items that we call the planets. The planets are nothing more than a storage facility for the raw materials that they created in the world's largest oven.

The questions I am asking you to realize are where did the stuff come from that the sun was made of? Where did the science come from that created the thermal nuclear bomb called the sun? Where did the essence come from that enabled the sun to have its physical essence and be able to burn the fuel with the rate it burns and be able to control and stay in a complete circle by itself and not implode or explode? This means it has to be magnetically controlled.

We have a bunch of space travelers, the extraterrestrials, who have the ability to create what we call the sun. All they know how to do evidently is put all the ingredients in a container area and then activate it and turn it into what we call the sun. The sun goes ahead and has this huge amount of power and all these rays and gases that it creates. Then it has to get rid of the debris or the discharge as we call it, right? So, this thing heats up for however many years or billions of years it takes for the motor to start burning and churning and making the liquid into a molten state of purity or pliability as you may call it. Then all of a sudden it reaches its peak at this time and it starts going pop, pop, pop, pop, pop and getting sick and spitting out these huge chunks as a coronal mass ejection. Sometimes the chunks are close together and sometimes they are not. Basically, the sun gets sick like that and goes through the process of the recycling and rendering down as it renders each of the contents that it makes. It goes through this big heater and transforms everything from the raw ingredients that they put into it to be transformed by this amazing huge oven, the biggest forge and fire ever created. These end up becoming the planets, okay. So, let us look at it as if the sun has just now hatched its own babies as we are going to call the planets to basically watch over and shine its light on them because you have to have light.

The sun was created by the extraterrestrials to produce the planets, right. Now if that is the case and it seems logical as they were created and manufactured for a certain reason and purpose. All I am simply going to say here is that without all of the other suns in space as we know it we would not have any light to able to see if there are any other solar systems for planets would we. Now one more time, if it was not for the suns being in all the different solar systems in our galaxy if we did not have suns towed or placed into the space where we have them we would not be able to see the other planets out there. We would not know that there are any other planets or solar systems. You cannot see the dark, right? Okay, so logically we are going to say from then, wait a minute, wouldn't that mean that the suns had to be_manufactured and put in a certain place so they would have a certain purpose and have a reason for being there, okay.

The sun was created to create the planets that it has produced. Think about the sun as a purifier and when it gets done it produces the rocks and pebbles where we live. That is just the way it is. Where would you consider the planets coming from if not coming from inside the sun? Where could you assemble them? How would you get them so hot? How could you get them so far away from the sun if you did not have a huge pressure cooker type spew that came out of it? You want to know some secret art? The best art I would like to see is when the sun basically created all the planets. Now that is not the big bang. Oh no, no, no. That is not the big bang when the sun basically spit out the planets. That is not the big bang at all. The original big bang is what actually created the essence that allowed the extraterrestrials to put the stuff inside the pressure cooker and find out the results.

The sun is the largest body in our solar system. Ask yourself the most simplistic question of all where else could the planets come from? If not from the sun then you are telling me we towed these planets into their place. Maybe we should realize that we towed the sun in place like it is the universe all sun the same way as the moon is the universe all canteen. How about that? A sun that you can tow into place or build into place and then create a solar system.

You have to realize and understand sometimes and just step back to see the larger picture. You never know when you see the complete picture because it is very seldom that we do. It is just hard to realize or be able to fantasize or understand that the sun itself is like a mother guarding her children. It was created to get hot to produce and create the planets which were eventually put in orbit out there and later to be harvested by people coming by and_mining from whatever they thought they needed from that planet. It is just hard to basically realize that we are nothing more than a mining solar system that has extraterrestrials that know how to do this process a whole lot better than we do. It just makes you wonder about all that, but you have to really think about the sun as a very unique manufactured item because it has to be.

How can you have so many suns out there that go ahead and all are burning bright and can burn for millions of years according to what we know, right? It can burn for all those periods of time. This big picture must be super big. All I am simply saying in the long and short of it is that the sun creates. The sun was created to create the planets that it has produced.

If we are not educated, then ninety-nine percent of us will never understand that this solar system is nothing more than a huge mining colony facility that provides goods for everybody else in all the other solar systems as well as other dimensions. So when we transcend then maybe that is when we have a chance to go to the next Promised Land that is called reality. When you break everything down to the basics then you start to realize and understand the essence of life, cosmic consciousness, and things of that nature. When you learn to treat everything with equal respect is when you rise above the spooze of humanity and really become a human instead of an uneducated individual.

You have to really think about the sun as a very unique manufactured item because it has to be. The sun is a creator. The sun was created to create the planets that it has produced. Then as they cool evidently the miners come in and do their process from one end to the other on the planets they desire to mine. I guess you have to really understand that each planet has its own basically primary signature of the elements that are on it by its periodic table of elements. So, each planet would have to be studied and tested to see what they would have on it. If they have the right things on them then you can basically send a biological spray of acids and oozes and stuff and start basic life until you get there and take advantage of what had already been created thousands or millions of years before earlier than you so when you get there you have control over them. Nowhere in the Bible does it say we have control over things in space. That might be a different way to look at things.

What is the point of the sun being the sun? It is already hot enough. Now what you have is the rendering down and refining of what we call the planets that are spit out in certain areas. Because they are a solid mass, they basically consistently have what you call mass density which provides the orbit that takes place. It is funny as it happens that these things are so hot for so long it makes you wonder that if they had what we term and call now a coronal mass ejection. This might be after the original ejection has happened or taken place one, two, or three times in the same area. This is discussed in more detail in the chapter about coronal mass ejection.

All of the planets are illuminated by the sun so we can see them. In the Bible it says I give you light so we think the light is for us to see with and we appreciate that. We use light to see with but we never imagine until you slow yourself down and think that very simply giving us light allowed us to be able to see the other planets, the other stars, and the other things that allowed us to stimulate our thinking. Without the sun in space giving light to everything basically then you would not know space existed. It would just be totally dark, right. No light so you would not know to go on adventures. If you are trapped in a cave and you are trying to find the way out and you do not know where the hole is as soon as you see the light you would scramble to it. The same thing we do with our intelligence and stupidity. We do not even know how to educate ourselves correctly yet but we try to. It is only what they will allow us to be educated with.

It has to be a manufactured type of engine that is out there to illuminate the stars and all that so we can see to travel and to wonder beyond our own selves. So anyway, redundancy is the way to find truth in reality because if you see it more and more and more you pay attention to it, right. So, if that is the case how could you ever see all the planets out there in the solar system without the sun out there illuminating like a lightbulb for us to see? It just makes me wonder about our dimension that we live in that we call it our reality. It might be our reality, but I still think that we have not really seen the true place of our fortune or after this premature or primary attempt at life like that we have here now. Maybe if we prove ourselves worthy enough we will be granted a second or third time of lifecycle because we add to the collectiveness of the universal consciousness that we have in the world which is universal respect. Once you learn how to travel through the universe through universal respect to become and be born alive again then you have proved yourself worthy through God and the people that have manufactured you. Not a bad way. Anyway, always light in your eyes and look forward to seeing you sometime in the future.

They have never studied the sun to ever think that the sun might actually tilt forward or backward or from side to side or up and down and turn left and right to basically roll around this material that is in its inner belly so it could be basically reduced down like in a kettle or a pot like you make soap. In other words to get it down to its essence you have to heat it up so hot that these things bond together. Now here again think about it when you bond all these materials together what is the point of the extraterrestrials even bothering to do this? So here again you never know what we could create given the proper environment. We could create a new periodic table of elements or a new type of pressure regulation and the math would be astronomically great on all this type of stuff.

What if the sun does have to go around and around moving itself in order to keep heating up what is inside, okay? There again lies the rub with the sun moving around. The sun rolls around with its pitching and rolling and swirling to mix it all up, right? So, what makes us so vain and blind is what if the sun sprays towards other planets but we are not paying attention to it. So do our scientists ever have a way of monitoring if any of the other planets have ever been sprayed before or does the sun just spray the residue of what is inside towards the planets

Earth, Mars, and the Asteroid Belt which are in the center of our solar system? Now it is just one of those scientific questions that I do not have the answer to. I am sure that there are a lot of people who have not thought of it. If you do not mix it up then how are you ever going to have any spray or anything? Remember the only reason the sun put the planets out there is that it got hot enough to where it actually sneezed or whatever you want to call a coronal mass ejection and put us all out here in all different shapes and sizes and forms.

What excites me is the thought that the sun is actually not only just being a sun sitting there as a brilliant light bulb but actually to have to roll itself over like a gyroscope again and again and again allowing itself to mix up the atomic fuel to keep it alive and keeping it spinning onward on itself. We have never actually studied the sun enough that I know of where this phenomenon has been proved or disproved. In other words what I am saying is that the sun actually has to have a way to stir the raw materials that are inside the pot. In the end before it goes supernova or when it does go supernova where do those remnants go? How valuable are those remnants when the sun emits them and goes supernova and explodes into itself and becomes a neutron star? The density factor of the residue that was left over from the sun after it used all of its atomic fuel is unbelievable.

Here again how do you get that much fuel to put inside that large of a mass? We thought the Ark was a big thing to build to hold all the animals. My goodness folks, can you imagine the science and technology it would take to go ahead and to put enough mass materials in an area to be able to conceal it and contain it and to walk away and hit it like it is a remote controlled detonation thing as we leave in our jet spacecraft, okay? There again when it starts igniting and building itself in a whirlwind of explosions and detonations as it makes more energy the electrical field in which it encapsulates itself becomes stronger and stronger until the sun cannot make it spin any longer and retain its gravity field of consistency and then it goes supernova dark star. I am not really sure yet. So that is a tremendous thing that would be great for me to understand about the sun. How long do you think it would last? How long have others lasted in the past?

How does the sun keep burning if it does not have oxygen? It is self-contained, isn't it? Now here again we never thought if the sun uses any of space as a fuel? Think about it. What does the sun do with all that space? Actually that space could be some kind of a gravitational field that holds the sun in place and holds the planets in place. I do not think so but it is very possible. It could be if you really think about it. You could look at the sun and all the planets as a point of reference that you would bounce off to create a gravity type of field from one point to another point to another point just like a telecommunications satellite so you can have a continual signal. Why wouldn't you do the same thing with the sun and the planets?

Let's look at it this way. Let's look at our solar system as a planetary electrical lock and each planet holds every other planet in place. That is basically the truth, isn't it? If not, why wouldn't the last planet just drift off in space? That is an interesting point of view. So actually, if you think about it, couldn't it happen this way? That may be. The planets keep the sun in check and the sun cannot escape the planetary grasp of all the children that it has created. Interesting point of view. It just goes to show you that everybody comes from somewhere but where is that place.

If you think about it from a magnetic point of view it is possible that all the planets going around the sun could magnetically keep it in its place there, right. So, what makes the sun to be in the exact center of all these planets that came out of it if it was not the origin in which they were born from or existed from? In other words all the planets used to be part of the sun. Bingo! What makes you think the sun was not purposely put where it was? Where did the sun originate from?

I cannot understand how once you would set it in process how you can already create a magnetic lock for the sun. The only way you can actually make a magnetic lock that would work for the sun is as the engine became more volatile and produced more energy so it would basically spin the magnetic motor or whatever it is in a generating fashion or stature to where it would automatically create the gravity field around it that would allow it to maintain. In other words, the faster the sun creates the more it encases itself in its own containment shield. There is a way to do it so then you might have a chance to sneak in the shielding if you wanted to go inside and do things.

Now here again if redundancy becomes logic and logic becomes fact then how many suns are out there that are doing the same thing as our sun is doing for us? Are you trying to get me to realize that we have a natural phenomenon that can control nuclear eruptions inside of a sphere and keep them contained there for millions of years producing all these lights and everything else? If there is nobody out there, then why are we wasting all these potential energy resources and products? Somebody did not start them up on fire without a reason. Remember fire? Okay, ask yourself this point of view how does the sun start its spark that allows it to initiate the total catastrophic or total combustion that takes place in the sun with millions of degrees? It has to heat everything up and purify it and then once it is purified until it cannot reduce it down any more like making lye soap. So there again when the sun gets as hot as it can handle and when it cannot stand it anymore then basically spits it out into the atmosphere causing planets and other solar systems to go through the same things we are doing.

The sun's creation as they say is the eruption of the nuclear bomb stuff that it takes to get to the hot degrees of Kelvin and everything that it takes that I do not even understand and have not studied to give you enough proper terminology other than it is just too damn hot for us to get to really. So, it would be hard for me to imagine that once you start this engine motor in process right, once you start the sun it is like an engine and a motor in process except it has no governor as such. How do you go ahead and know the way this thing is going to molt and turn things over and basically flip it and do this and do that?

So anyway, we need to find out how you would create such a huge large nuclear motor that is a thousand times larger than the size of the planets. Think about the mass and the size of the sun to do the math. The sun has a diameter of 864,340 miles. Then you go ahead and have the sun spit out all these planets, okay. What is the diameter of these different planets? The planet Earth has a diameter of 7,919.5 miles and the largest planet Jupiter has a diameter of 86,881 miles. So there again none of the planets are even close to being the diameter of the sun itself, right. What if we added up the diameters of all of the planets, would that total equal the diameter of the sun?

Let's think about the possibility that the sun is replaceable like a light bulb is replaceable. Now ask yourself how can that be possible? The sun is replaceable. Well you have to listen to what I am saying to understand that is an amazing situation. The reason is to come to the simple understanding of what you see in the complete cycle of the yin and yang. It is basically easy to be understood and the secrets are revealed so what I am saying right now because I know nothing before I start the process.

So, if you really think about it the sun does what it does and every once in a while the sun basically as it goes through its period of time and goes through a destructive cycle which they call a super nova or neutron star or something of that nature. Again, here the funny part of it is when the neutron star yields all its yield and cannot handle it anymore it explodes, right, and it wipes out everything that is in that solar system. Does that allow us to realize and understand and envision very simply you get to start all over again by bringing in a new sun and start it all over again?

You know you can have another solar system in the exact same place we have had this one in space just like we can rebuild the town in the same place the town was in before. You just have to see the grand picture and scheme of things. It is like a yin and yang thing. The thing that it creates also destroys it. So the only way to really escape life in a new realization to learn how to really escape life is to learn how to leave the solar system before the sun goes supernova or to know here is the quest when it is going to go supernova to get the hell out of Dodge. Now that is the way to go and everybody knows that so instead of a 2012 type of thing have just a spray on the planets which would not be as devastating if the sun decides to just explode instead.

Scientists say they know how to study the sun to see when it is degrading and is going to blow and when it is not going to blow. But you know honestly, I do not think we have been alive long enough to really know anything about the sun unless we are sharing knowledge with the extraterrestrials about this topic. They would know more about the sun than_we do because they created the sun. They have had more time to study it than we have.

It is the God's truth. We know nothing compared to what we are going to know in a thousand years from now, right. So here again what do we know from a thousand years in the past. Very little. We know some. I should say about five thousand years in the past instead of being literal just being general, okay. But here again I am trying to just make it purely understood that the sun is just like a human being. It does its thing but I have never really realized and did not understand it that the sun and all the planets and everything could be nothing more than a huge mining colony for everybody else like I have said earlier. It is really a funny point of view. I think I am being redundant and all this time.

I did not say that I know everything about the universe. But I do know what is right and what is wrong. What is logical and what is not. God said let there be light and there was light. We always assume the light was just for us here on our own planet. We never think we would look up at the stars and ask where did that light come from? Here you want to know a real funny part of it is look at how many stars are out there that give us light, points of light that we can basically what would you call plot a course on the way. So, stars are nothing more than street signs. That is all that they are. They are way stations for the travelers just like stagecoaches having a place to put their stuff in and get whatever they need if that is the case. Anyway until we get back there and see it all again we do not know what is in our own mind because if you keep the light of education from your own self then you are doomed to darkness and repetition of not knowing and being confused and always frustrated. I would just like to see everybody not be frustrated and to understand I guess because that is my goal in life to remove all the miscommunication and misunderstanding between people so there is perfect communication and there is no communication breakdown.

You are looking for the light. You know, trying to connect the dots or trying to be educated. We are trying to do all these things but you have to slowly realize and remember that without light we could not see. Without light we would not exist. Without the sun we cannot exist because our bodies need the Vitamin D and stuff from the sun. If it was not for light where would we be? The answer is obvious. We would not be and we could not be. That is the truth. Without light we do not exist.

You have to also remember that without the sun you cannot create human people in the way we are today. Think about it that way. What we are saying right now about the sun is that we realize when God says in the Bible in the book of Genesis that he created the heavens and the Earth. He created Earth and the heavens, okay. What that means to me is that he created the universe in the shape that it is in and created not only the other planets but the sun, okay. So that is correct and we agree that he created the heavens and the Earth, the sun and the stars also. So what we are saying exactly is that he cultivated the heavens and the Earth and he also made the sun, right.

To summarize: the sun is the world's largest forge in the sky and is the hugest oven that produces the planets and the elements in the planets. Here again you would think that maybe all the elements here would work with the sun. We have come to understand that the sun will wipe itself out again so the whole situation starts over again with the yin and yang scenario allowing the sun to go supernova so it completely destroys and wipes out the solar system allowing for a new situation to take place. It is always a recycle just as birth and rebirth all over again in the yin and yang complex except with the suns out there how would they ever know to stack raw materials in all and how much would they put in them and how would they do what they do. They know basically the extrapolation after the planets have cooked and become a molten mass and become a discharge point where they can start cooling and forming into the planets. It is all a manufacturing process that they have done probably millions of times before being however many solar systems there are.

Remember just because we see the solar systems now does not it mean that there have not been two or three solar systems in that same location that have gone through the turnstile cycle that allows them to be totally evacuated when the sun goes supernova. There again they come right back in the same situation and do the same thing all over again. So how would you ever have a magnetic lock that would allow you to have all those raw materials to get together and then turned into a creation pit and pot that you would go ahead and be able to condense and keep this field around to where it would blow itself apart? There again should tell you that the sun itself has to be mechanically manufactured so it will not tear itself apart. Nobody can control nuclear explosions, right, so how can the sun control nuclear explosions and keep them contained inside of a light bulb area.

You know it is like a light bulb inside of a light bulb area. That is exactly what the sun is. We have no outer area to keep ourselves from the shielding. That is what the sun's rays do. They go through that barrier. There has to be a magnetic field around the sun, something to contain it, its own gravity. You want to believe that is the case and then the sun could also create a gravitational field. We know it creates a density field. We know that it takes more mathematics than we understand to create a sphere that would hold everything inside that you could not go back and ever touch and research that I know of. That does not mean it is not possible. There is always a back door to get to the treasure. Think about it.

You have to realize and understand sometimes and just step back to see the larger picture. You never know when you see the complete picture because it is very seldom that we do. It is just hard to realize or be able to fantasize or understand that the sun itself is like a mother guarding her children. It was created to get hot to produce and create the planets which were eventually put in orbit out there and later to be harvested by people coming by and mining from whatever they thought they needed from that planet so it was just a realization of everything. It is just hard to basically realize that we are nothing more than a mining solar system that has extraterrestrials that know how to do this process a whole lot better than we do. It just makes you wonder about all that.

You have to really think about the sun as a very unique manufactured item. How can you have so many suns out there that go ahead and all are burning bright and can burn for millions of years according to what we know, right? It can burn for all those periods of time. This big picture must be super big. All I am simply saying in the long and short of it is that the sun creates. The sun was created to create the planets that it has produced and as they cool then the miners come in and do the process from one end to the other on the planets that they desire to mine.

But here again I am not a scientist or anybody that studies science. This is just my opinion as an individually educated person on the topic. I am an independent study person. I do it for my own entertainment and I am trying to share what I believe is accurate and everybody else would like to know on the easy side of it. I call that being able to pick up a book and read it to make a summarized version of the last twelve or fifteen years of my life. Just think of it that way. But anyway, as you go through time it is funny how you have to step back and look at how you have spent the past years. You have to realize and understand sometimes and just step back to see the larger picture. You never know when you see the complete picture because it is very seldom that we do. May God bless you with the ability to connect the dots so you can see the light.

I know this is back to where we started in this chapter about the sun but it seems logical that where else can I go with this other than realizing that the sun is really a creation that does this not only in our solar system but in all these other solar systems. Now think of us not to see that if one solar system and all these other solar systems. Maybe that is what they are trying to do is keep creating new and better solar systems with new models and humans and design patterns and design features. Why not? It sounds logical. Why not? Then send us a rebuttal or contact us and tell us what you think about the book. There you go.

CHAPTER SIX

CORONAL MASS EJECTIONS

The Birth of the Planets

In the Bible in the book of Genesis it says God created heaven and earth and all. Right? Okay, now where did the planets come from? Do not say God created the planets. Well he might have but where did they come from even though he might have created them? Okay, all I am saying here is understand from this simple point of view that you have to have a point of origin. Right? Okay, what I am saying is that the point of origin here is the sun came to a point that it had a coronal mass ejection. The sun finally spit out at this time a coronal mass ejection to start our solar system. Okay now, instead of just being a coronal mass ejection what I am suggesting here is that it pushed a planet out or birthed a planet out of the sun. The sun was so hot and it had so much extra material inside that it formed a planet. The coronal mass ejection is just getting rid of something that it is sick of. It gets sick and spits it out like you or I would. It is the same type of thing.

Now the question here is who created the sun and knows it is going to spit this stuff out and create a solar system? It all has to be mathematically done or you could not have it produce a perfect mathematical situation. The extraterrestrials created the sun to produce the planets. They were created and manufactured for a certain reason and purpose. The sun produced the planets through a coronal mass ejection therefore creating our solar system. Coronal mass ejected planets.

The sun probably had a coronal mass ejection and it finally spit out a planet to start the solar system. Now instead of just being a coronal mass ejection it pushed a planet out or birthed a planet because it was so hot and had so much extra material inside that it could form a planet. Look at how large the sun is and how hot the sun is to create large molting masses of such size. Because the sun is so much larger than any of the planets therefore a coronal mass ejection is just getting rid of something that it is sick of and spits it out like you or I would do. It is the same thing.

So, if we keep going on about where the planets come from you have to eventually tie yourself back into everything with realizing the egg shape and form of life and birth. We keep hearing that everybody is born from an egg. Let's also imagine that the planets were born from an egg. I am just going to take the egg shape and form a little farther and bring it to bear more fruit in a science fiction kind of way. Why couldn't you consider the sun to be a large egg and everything came from it because it created more eggs from within itself? Now would that not be a strange place? Where did the egg come from? Well, the egg came from inside of its own self. An egg in front of an egg. So actually, what I am trying to say is that the sun could be a large egg and the planets are its children. It is just another way of looking at it in a funny way of understanding.

The sun to me is the mother that birthed all the planets. Therefore, I am going to the next step and connecting the dots to say that the planets are actually the eggs that allowed everything and the birth to be done from them. As well as you could consider the egg to be the sun itself and therefore these are the children from within it. Is God the sun? Is Mother Nature the sun? Is Father Nature the sun and everything that it creates? The question I have is who created the sun? Where did they all come from? That is too much to bite on from this point of view. I guess I will have to come and take myself to the extraterrestrial library so I can understand it.

One thing that I left out of here is that the sun could be called a birth canal. Now think about that. It is a birthing canal for the planets. The planets had to be birthed through a birthing canal or some area and remember the good shot could also be what we call the birthing canal or being pushed out of it. It is just one of those types of things you ponder about. You will never know the proper terminology unless you keep trying. So therefore, what I am trying to say to you is that the sun could have birthed these planets as a coronal mass ejection.

So anyway, the planets are out there in the solar system and all. Right? But how did they get there? What established the orbits of the planets and the order of the planets? What I am saying is that when the planets were made they were shot out of the sun. The sun ejected each planet as a coronal mass ejection. All I know to call it is that a planet was ejected by the sun starting the creation of our solar system.

Everybody keeps calling it the Big Bang. What if the Big Bang was a coronal mass ejection except it had a planet in it that had yet to fall into its natural place in the solar system? I was wondering if the Big Bang could be associated with the formation of the planets of the solar system. The noise it would make from the sun giving birth as if it was the egg to all these other lower eggs which we call planets. That is just the way it goes, isn't it?

The sun is the mother of all of the planets because it is the only possibility for the hugest biggest heater motor oven to produce the product. In other words, you do not fall too far from where the product was made usually. You have heard the expression the apple does not fall far from the tree relating to a son or a daughter and their parents. This is in the same concept of thought. But what I am asking you to realize here is that even though the sun did its deal and I believe that every period of time it had to go through its evolutionary state of purging the sickness from it. A coronal mass ejection is what we would call it.

Basically having a sick stomach if you get sick or vomit is what we call a mass ejection. You get chunks in your vomit when you get sick so just imagine that those chunks happen to be planets and all the chunks came from within an area like your stomach and then as you would go to get sick you would expel it from your system. That is the same thing that the sun did with the planets here. It had to be. There is no other way that anything can come along with this size of the planets and be able to purge them out into space.

Coronal mass ejections could also be considered a cough or a sneeze so you can understand it but the grandeur and the size of it is just astronomical. You understand because the sneezing of the sun or the coughing of the sun are just words for what is called a coronal mass ejection. Those words might be here just to confuse you if you want to track the scientific wonder of the terminology but it is just like a cough or a hack or a sneeze, you know, or even blowing your nose. A coronal mass ejection is the same thing. So, do not be confused by the terminology.

It is no big deal. It is just we have to do it for you to finally have to come to the understanding of what really does happen. It is what the game is all about. So imagine in your mind of being a natural scientist as the planet cooled slower and slower it is still spinning around and around because the action inside the sun had to mix all the natural chemicals and everything up and the other stuff settles to the bottom and you have to dispense it. When it is dispensed it spins depending on how many times the sun got sick and where it got sick and therefore the chunks all spun off and made all the little smaller planets. We do not know for sure and me being uneducated I can only assume and put together the natural flow of how I would have it done so it could not be destroyed any other way than the way nature tells you to do things. So if you follow nature's course you will never be lost. You will never fail. You just have to understand the true course of nature and then you will achieve your task and goal.

We were saying, discussing, and rambling on about how the sun has an upset stomach is one way for you to understand it termed as a coronal mass ejection. So what we are saying is simply that the planets are spewed out at one time into the solar system once in the beginning and once in the end to develop them all as they are spun out. This might be the most logical reasonable answer of all is that a large amount was spewed out from the sun in large chunks or whatever size chunks or however it got divided up. Let's assume that it was thrown out into space itself. As it cooled down and those pieces got harder then, as I understand heat and cold, as the outside got cold and the inside was still hot eventually it would cease spinning. Then you would have a chunk which we call a planet that would be thrown off away from the center mass. This would allow the next part of the outside skin to harden and therefore in a circular motion be slung off of the huge ball in the center. This would create whichever planet in whatever size and allow it to cool and have density.

We know one thing. The planets are here in the solar system and we are on them. Somebody or something originally had to start the sun and keep it that way. Did the planets all come out at one time in a single coronal mass ejection? They all could have come out at the same time in a single spew and in a spiralization as the solar system. The planets were all spewed out at one time. What might be the most logical reasonable answer of all is that a large amount was spewed out from the sun in large chunks. As they cooled down and the pieces got harder then, as I understand heat and cold, as the outside got cold and the inside was still hot eventually they would cease spinning and there would be a chunk which we call a planet. This would allow the next part of the outside skin to harden and in a circular motion be slung off of the huge ball in the center therefore creating whichever planet of whichever size allowed it to cool and have as much density.

So with understanding the hours and hours and days and days and years and years about why and how the planets became where they are and how they are it is a simple manifestation of cultivating your mind and asking if you were a large mass and you got sick how many times do you get sick and spit something out of yourself that would cause you to spit it out. If we use the clock as a reference at what time and what place did the sun spit it out? There again evidently since there are nine or ten planets in the solar system it got sick either nine or ten times.

The only thing that I do not really know or have not had a chance to study is the point of view of how many planets were ejected at what time or percentage rate. Were the ejections spread out over a period of time? Did they all come out in a matter of months or weeks or years? Did they all cool together in their orbits so they could magnetically hold their own orbit? Or were they produced one at a time? Or as one was produced then the next one came in line and waited to define its orbit in the solar system. This basically leads me to believe that the sun is running out of material inside it to keep the sun hot. This is very logical.

If the sun spins around and around at that speed with the power and push of it you could say that the coronal mass ejection was almost like a gunshot going off and projecting the bullet which would have been the planet and creating our solar systems. Now here again the logical point of understanding and all is did all the planets come out at one, two, three, four, five, six, seven, eight, nine and even more are farther out there or was it a controlled effort of one and then it started to cool and a second and it started to cool? Did they haystack the planets one at a time or they all come out into space at a different period of time in the orbits so they would consistently not bump into each other and make their orbit or their order pattern of circulation around the sun?

Most people miss the important fact that there is no other place in our solar system or space where the hugest, the largest creation of all is heat and pressure. Therefore the only logical conclusion is the sun and the coronal mass ejections that we have now were once a coronal mass ejection that spit out or produced hot molten planets that started their own planetary ring which had to be solid at one time to definitely make the solar system the size it is and the planets having the orbit that they have. So therefore to be logical in the way of processing it would seem that most of these planets would have to have been ejected from the sun in a mathematical time of placing so as they cool down as they went around the sun they would basically form into a perfect circular union around the sun. It is very important that all the planets are in a circular motion around the sun now. How can that be if they did not come from it? So something outside the sun had to come in and then set the planets in place and leave? No, no, no. No, if you go against nature you just get nah, nah, nah. But if you go with nature and say yes then yes is logical. The sun being as big as it is could have gone through this process which means the sun itself was manufactured to create planets. I know that is a hard step for you to realize. But then again, the leftover residue that was in the sun itself at a certain period of time spit out the planets which created our solar system. That is where they came from. There is no logical way you can have all these mass molten blobs going around in a circular motion such as the sun having a gravitational pull. Also, the amount of density each planet had would determine the orbit of how the planets came into being by the density going to the farthest out.

Basically, as we were talking we said that as the planets were being formed they were spit out in some kind of similar time and in some kind of similar motion for them to have a chance to exist. In other words, even though they had not cooled yet they still had density and mass which allowed them to basically move around and create their orbits. What I seem to be funny at understanding is if you have these planets and all these different places and it takes all this different time for the orbits to be in years or months or however long it takes to go around the sun, well then it seems funny that you missed the idea that the planets go around the sun because it has a gravitational pull to it. So therefore, in the orientation where did it come from? How could it not come from the inside out? The sun is spinning around and around and around and slinging this stuff out. So, the question is does the sun spin and how fast does it go around and around?

The whole point in the focus of my curiosity that I do not seem to be able to get a handle on now is that for all these planets to develop an orbit and maintain this orbit it seems to me to be only logical that these planets at some time had to be basically what you would call I guess extruded from the sun itself and put in space creating our solar system. The solar system was not here until the planets arrived. Then I guess the heating and the density of the planets was what basically determined the orbit of the planets so therefore you have to have density to have a planet formed in orbit.

What keeps bothering me about the coronal mass ejection from the sun is why does it always seem to be on a time lock or a time zone in which somebody can predict when it is going to happen again like the Mayans did? See that means that it is mathematical and it is probably man-made or human made or intelligently manufactured for a purpose. Like I said, now we realize that the whole solar system could be nothing more than a huge mining experience. What a great way to go that we live in a mining solar system. Talk about putting yourself in a class distinction. You could say we are one of many planets that help go ahead and provide for the main planet like the worker bees providing for the queen bee. Now let's take it to the next step further and say all the planets give what they produce to the supreme planet. It is the same thing. You are always giving yourself. You just do not realize it. Look at how easy youth gives itself away to age.

The sun shot the farthest planet out first and let's say that it had a chance to start cooling for twenty-six thousand years. That one planet could have started the solar system. If we are correct then every twenty-six thousand years the sun went through the process of having a coronal mass ejection and producing another planet. Every twenty-six thousand years another planet would be ejected and go as far as it could and all of a sudden there would be a gravity field there because the density of the planet was there and therefore hay stacking and creating planets with the newest ones coming closer and closer to the sun. This is just a very logical possibility of why they are here now.

Could the twenty-six thousand years cycle of alignment of the planets be the only time that the sun spits out a coronal mass ejection? This would be something to wonder about. We know that the alignment happens at least every twenty-six thousand years. It only makes sense that a coronal mass ejection happens or takes place every twenty-six thousand years to be in a mathematical cycle. I do not understand where every twenty-six thousand years that one of the planets in the solar system gets sprayed upon by a coronal mass ejection from the sun. Now that is a new one that I just came up with. You talk about not a bad way to think about it. Anyway, it is just one of those things. Coronal mass ejections might be targeting in a mathematical process to destroy all the planets it once created through the first ejection of all the planets that were expelled from the sun. And from then on out it did not have the extra debris inside to create a planet ejection. It is just now a coronal mass ejection of gas and everything else inside. Interesting take but it sort of makes sense doesn't it?

What makes sense with the record of the coronal mass ejection so long ago is that the planets were all put out here one at a time which is my best guesstimate. I am being instructed that what basically happened is that the planets were spewed out of the sun and therefore basically jumbled and tumbled around to make the orbits as they were once established and founded. Therefore as we go through this then at some time and some basis the Earth was turned into its time clock to where they could monitor every twenty-six thousand years when basically a coronal mass ejection is going to happen in the solar system. Now my question beyond that is very possibly does each planet go through a one time coronal mass ejection as it is near the end of the sun to where it would have an effect or does the sun have a coronal mass ejection on a different planet every twenty six thousand years? In other words, does it spew out of the sun always in the same place or does it change as the sun gets older and the spew comes out closer and closer to the planets that it created? Here you have the perfect Yin and Yang complex again as you see as it emits it and puts them out as originally in shape and fortune and in place and everything.

Then at some time somebody had to basically understand or know ahead of time that there was going to still be a pressure release valve in the sun which we call coronal mass ejection which would spray on one planet or would always just spray on planet Earth. So, is the coronal mass ejection of the sun always focused at planet Earth or would it change with the age of it by going to a basically different planet to put it in harm's way? The reason I ask this is to understand basically that this situation could easily have happened on Mars and the fifth ring planet.

Here again what bothers me about the twenty-six thousand years cycle of precession is that you need to calculate how many times it has occurred before someone decided to pay attention and study it. That is what leads me to believe that the planets may have been made every twenty-six thousand years so therefore you can actually have a date in which you could actually put a time on how long it took to make our solar system. You push one planet out and it goes as far away as it can and in the next twenty-six thousand years is the same thing because the outer planet has had a chance to cool. Maybe just possibly it has created the outermost planet that developed and started all the other planets to have stopped with their ejection before the planets become closer and closer. So here again it would lead us to understand that the coronal mass ejections are able to be studied by the civilizations after they knew they came at a certain period of time. It seems as if they made a time clock of earth that the twenty-six thousand years period is the time in which this thing goes off.

What I think is a basic thing if you will pay attention is how did all the planets happen to be there at a certain time in a certain distance spread apart so they could allow themselves to develop an orbit for the planet? Now listen to this again, how can you have all the planets come out at different times which you could not have every twenty-six thousand years or then the planets would not be able to produce an orbit? Now if this was the case you can do it one planet at one time then the second, third, fourth, fifth, sixth planet in a row if you were able to control the expelling of the coronal mass ejection into space. So therefore it allows me to come up with the answer that they all had to be spit out at a certain period of time at a certain distance apart which means it had to be mathematically done to make a mathematical solar system with the orbits perfectly round or elliptical basically going to go ahead and allow them to exist.

A coronal mass ejection could have been what was supposed to happen at 2012. It had happened probably twenty-six thousand years earlier. We do not know but it had to happen pretty much the same time over and over again for them to be able to study it and record it and pass it on into history, right? What is the situation with the sun now since the 2012 anomaly did not really destroy our planet because it basically got a pass for some reason? Either the extraterrestrials put a pass on it or this is the last time a coronal mass ejection did not have a perfect alignment and missed us. I believe this is probably the proof that the coronal mass ejection missed planet Earth. Either it was earlier or it was later but it did miss us.

Now remember that somebody somewhere had to know that in 2012 this coronal mass ejection was going to happen because it happened every twenty-six thousand years. So, we are assuming possibly in the nature of things that each of these planets in our solar system has gone through a coronal mass ejection contamination of being spewed on possibly to cause it to be destroyed. Or is it just every twenty-six thousand years that the coronal mass ejection spews on planet Earth, Mars, and the fifth ring planet and finally destroyed one of them with a perfect shot of coronal mass ejection? Was this mass ejection at 2012 just for the planet Earth this time or is the next planet on down the line having its coronal mass ejection? You never know when or where the coronal mass ejection will spray on which planet. There again lies the reason for everybody on every planet to be aware of this and to take it into consideration. But I still like the idea that the planet Earth is the timer or the clock that initiates when this coronal mass ejection was going to happen. Now if it transfers to the next planet in line and there again we will have to pay attention and try to find out how that planet lines up with a mathematical possibility for a coronal ejection at twenty-six thousand years to spray on what planet.

Also was the planet Earth made to be a time clock so that every twenty-six thousand years the alignment comes around and some way, some reason, somehow, somebody knew that the coronal mass ejection was going to happen and destroy everybody but nobody until 2012 even knew or put their mind around the concept. So there again ask yourself would this be enough time for the ancients to be able to see how long it takes for the sun to eject or push a planet out.

Yet no one ever understands that the 2012 anomaly was either a twenty-six thousand years cycle or it was the thing of electronic release of the magnetism going through electronical flux or something like that. But here again you tell me where else could have been a more logical place for the planets to have been produced from other than a form of a nuclear Easy Bake Oven™ in the stars. You tell me if you can come up with a better idea. And you have all the solar systems come out and all the solar systems have a sun and you do not think it was mathematically created here for some reason. Just because we do not have the imagination and brains to be able to realize we do not know.

If you think about the coronal mass ejection, then 2012 was just a spew and everything of that nature that we missed because of the timing was off two or three days or whatever. It makes you wonder how many times in the past it has been just a spew of stuff instead of planets. Now I am trying to come up with the idea that maybe this thing was that the sun got sick at one time and emitted a coronal mass ejection because all the planets from the sun had to be molten when they were discharged. So therefore, the planets were all expelled at the same time like you would when you get sick from having the wrong kind of stuff in your stomach. Then I guess it is only an assumption that from then on after the planets were dispersed into the solar system that we now inhabit that very possibly from then on it was only a coronal mass ejection that did not have any more extra debris in the sun's reservoir to spill out upon us in the shape of planets. So now what we do is spray everything with a coronal mass ejection spray instead of having physical density mass evidence come out such as planets and stuff.

You also have to realize that with the 2012 anomaly and this thing called the coronal mass ejection that no one ever really got through to you to say that is just what was going to happen. This coronal mass ejection was supposed to destroy Earth. Does this not seem to you logically that even though we had all the Mayans and others studying this for tens of thousands of years over and over again that, wait a minute, somehow some way somebody knew that this 2012 anomaly thing had to be time oriented where they would know what was going to happen? So the Mayans set up their clock. Then from there basically used it as a time clock for when it got back to zero the closest it could to the sun is when the coronal mass ejection happens. Now is this only for planet Earth or does this happen just because the sun created all the planets out here in the Yin and Yang world of complacency? It seems only logical in nature that the sun itself would basically have a chance at coronal mass ejecting on each one of these planets at a certain period of time. It is a very real possibility but I am not sure of that.

Some way, some reason, somehow, somebody had to know that the coronal mass ejection was going to happen and destroy everybody. But nobody until 2012 even knew or put their mind around the concept. So here again ask yourself would this be enough time for the ancients to be able to see how long it takes the sun to be able to eject or push a planet out. As far as what we call coronal mass ejection might be what is only leftover residue of the sun's energy source that it had back inside of it. Would it allow the sun to be bigger, brighter, and longer? And there again lies the reality of the sun being the mother of all the planets. If you allow yourself to think about the time in which it may have taken for the sun to eject all the planets and create our solar system. Think about the irony of someone actually being able to pay attention enough to monitor that it is every twenty-six thousand years. In other words, it is working longer and lasting longer once it spits the planet out. Anyway, what I am trying to realize and come to grips with is the amount of time it took for someone to know when to pay attention to this. Now in our world being as young as we are we would not know or have privy to any books that would say this is what happens when you have the unique sun out there. The sun does this, does that, and spits out the residue of what it cannot deal with and creates the planets there around it. Wouldn't that be unique? That is what really happens and there again lies the obvious truth if you can't see it then you don't know to look for it.

Getting back to the 2012 issue. Is there any way we can prove that this kind of event happened before the 2012 event? Is there any scientific way to prove it? I am sure there is a way to prove a coronal mass ejection happened twenty-six thousand years earlier than 2012. Now it is just one of those questions I have.

When the December 21, 2012 predicted destruction did not happen it upset me so severely that I wrote this book and had to dig deeper and deeper to find out just what happened. You have to ask if the next coronal mass ejection which is coming up in twenty-six thousand years or whenever will it once again spray upon planet Earth? Or does the coronal mass ejection every twenty-six thousand years have a new position that it sprays upon the planets because they are slowly drifting away from the sun and the coronal mass ejection happens? I do not know if it happens in the same spot or not. It seems logical that as the planet becomes closer to the sun that would initiate some kind of electrical lock, some kind of planetary mass that might allow it to initiate the contact that would allow it to cause a coronal mass ejection and destroy the planets.

Therefore, the Yin and Yang complex itself is creation and death by its own hand which is the hyena complex. The hyena complex is what I basically call a lot of things. If you cannot see that you are destroying your own self, then you are the hyena going to eat your own self at your own place. You just have to stop and see the logic of what you are doing sometime. What you have to realize and take into consideration is that none of the planets in our solar system are larger than the sun. So therefore, what I am trying to say to you is that the sun could have birthed these planets as a coronal mass ejection. Now if that has anything to do with the twenty-six thousand years cycle then every twenty-six thousand years the sun birthed a planet because of the extra residue it had in it. The residue to me is the planet being spit out into space itself and creating our solar system one planet at a time. In reality every planet that it spits out into space is a planet that could one day become fuel inside the sun when the sun starts running out of fuel. So basically, what we have here is a sun that starts going ahead and has these anomalies turn into coronal mass ejections.

Did the planets really come out one every twenty-six thousand years? Did they come out like a clock spinning around and around as the sun would get sick and spit it out a piece and a piece and a piece as you would if you had an upset stomach? Is this the way they basically were scattered into space creating a solar system and an orbit in which the planets reside? It is just an unknown question. It does not mean it cannot be answered. It just means we have to get the books that have been written that describe and reveal it to us all. This has been done before folks. You just have to wake up and realize it because the new crop on a new planet that is trying to understand and resource our originality for sanity in our mind so we will not go insane. I speak for myself I guess but here again if I have realized and created it then it is a great thing and a good thought and a good process then of maintaining the thought of the sanity within yourself. If I can do it then how come you cannot? Anybody can through the one word you do not hear which is discipline. Maybe I just did not know what I was doing and just ran free down the road and let the essence of the universe guide me to be what I am today.

We do not know for sure and me being uneducated I can only assume and put together the natural flow of how I would have done it so it could not be any other way than the way nature tells you to do things. So if you follow nature's course you will never be lost. You will never fail. So in order to understand the hours and days and years about why and how the planets became where and how they are is a simple manifestation of cultivating your mind and asking if you were a large mass how many times do you get sick and spit something out. If we use the clock as a reference at what time and what place did the sun spit it out? There again evidently since there are nine or ten planets in the solar system it got sick nine or ten times.

What I am saying is that each of the planets were pushed out into our solar system as having a certain amount of stuff in each planet therefore allowing it to cool in the orbit or create an orbit because of its density or wherever it was put into the orbit. I do not know but I do know that all the planets were basically formed from molten rocks or something of that nature which means that the orientation has to be somewhat close for all of them to be together and cool around the same time. I am not educated in that field so these are questions that I am asking you to help us answer.

Here again I think this might be a good answer to solving the problem of where the planets come from in one type point of view because that would lead everything to have an equal time to cool in the same area that it was and all these other different things. So therefore, I guess the density of the planet would determine where the proper I guess sorting process would take place because they all had to have density to create an orbit. And without the planet being dense if it was just a bunch of rocks and then the other larger planets through the point of mathematical density and volume would have compressed that orbit to where the fifth planet would not exist. It is just basic math and I am not even smart.

So there again coronal mass ejections I guess occurred only after the planets were dispensed to create the solar system that we have now. It is funny that the same stuff that made the planets was once the sun's fuel inside its own self. Therefore, when the sun goes out is a perfect example of the yin and yang that gave all the life in itself completely without end and now it is going basically to kill everything off that it created when it goes extinct and destroys the whole solar system. It is sort of wild of how you have to see the yin and yang of all possibilities and all mass things to understand it. It is called the pros and cons as you would call it in your world today. What are the pros and cons of doing this?

Now the other thing we are dealing with here is that the sun basically as it works and does its things daily that its coronal mass ejection thing is the perfect Yin and Yang thing. It destroys us all. I am repeating myself here that all the suns all over space if you think about it and look at the suns and then you look at their solar systems around them would it not seem logical that this was like a real estate situation. Then there again you go, have it over and over again that each new I guess life that they create has its own certain planet that it goes and inhabits.

So, what we are trying to do here is come to grips with how the planets are able to be spewed out of the sun and at what rate. Let's assume the sun got hot enough from the point of looking at it from a natural point of flow and simply say that the sun was ignited by the originators of the sun. The whole point of what we are trying to assess here and understand is that we do not know how the planets were spewed out. But if you look at it in a form of natural flow as the originators or initiators started the sun doing its thing as it began to come to a point of having to have the pressure release valve syndrome which we call a coronal mass ejection. I call it getting sick in your stomach in a gross form of being able to assimilate with what is really happening. Therefore, the sun got hot enough and was spinning around enough and ejected the planets as a coronal mass ejection.

The essence is what makes it all possible for the creation that we know. So, who ever created the essence there again that is the rub because they even created the sun that created the planets that created the solar system that created all of us to exist. So here again it is a trickle down science project. The sun is the largest essence creator of all. In other words, it deduces down to make the essence and then it spits it out creating the planets. Where did the essence come from that enabled the sun to have its physical essence and be able to burn the field at the rate it burns and be able to control and stay in a complete circle by itself but not explode or implode? This means that it has to be magnetically controlled.

It basically leads me to believe that the sun is running out of material to keep itself hot. This is a very logical thing. Therefore, lies the rub that maybe the natural cycle of our solar system and the sun is running out of its extra essence inside to create any more planets. Now the sun emits only a coronal mass ejection which is a bunch of gamma rays that are left over from stuff not being able to cook in the pot. All we have left now is heat and gas that is being spit out.

Logically if you were to ask yourself where did the planets come from what other logical answer could you come up with? Logic you say has no answer in this field. If you think that then you have already lost yourself because logic is what makes you ask questions, receive the answers, and ascertain the information for a better decision. Where else would the planets come from? How do you think all of the planets got here? What point would it be for the sun to all of a sudden have a coronal mass ejection and produce another planet? What would the scientists think if the sun produced another planet now and shot it out into our solar system? Now that would be a wild one! That would really blow everybody up. I never thought about it until right   now.

CHAPTER SEVEN

THE ASTEROID BELT PLANET
The Fifth Planet

The asteroid belt or the fifth planet as I call it is a ring of asteroids or rocks located in an orbit between the planets Mars and Jupiter. The asteroid belt was a planet at one time but it was destroyed and is now ring of rocks. We know that a planet was there at one time because of the distances between the orbits of the other planets in the solar system. It had to be there to establish the orbits of the other this planets and the density and the gravity of developing our solar system. That is just the way it had to work.

The question is why was the planet destroyed and how was the planet destroyed? Did the planet explode? How did the planet explode? How many times could it have exploded? Did a rock hit the planet and cause it to explode into pieces? Was it a sonic weapon? Did some type of a nuclear motor explode the planet into pieces? Was it a natural disaster of some type? The asteroid planet could have been destroyed by either one of several different things.

One way it could have been destroyed was a rock hit the fifth planet and caused it to explode. However, it seems very unlikely that a rock would hit the planet and totally destroy it into a thousand pieces. If a rock hit the planet so hard to knock it into pieces then its pieces would have been knocked way out of its gravitational field and knocked all over the universe. Therefore the rocks would have been displaced and not been contained in the asteroid belt. You cannot take something that solid and hit it with another rock without it chipping into all these little rocks and they go everywhere in space. Besides how many pieces would stick around in the orbit? In other words, if a rock had hit the asteroid so hard that it exploded then the pieces would have been scattered so far out in space that they would not have been left in the orbit that is now the asteroid belt. So that is why the rock episode does not work. So, something else had to happen.

Why are all of the asteroids in the asteroid belt in chunks and pieces and round? I am not really educated on this a whole lot but the asteroid belt does not seem to have any huge chunks versus small chinks. I know that there are different sizes possibly. But if there are not any different sizes and they are all unified in size, then it was destroyed by a way to carve it up perfectly. I do not think that a sonic blast would have caused all of the pieces to be small and even sized. But here again it could have been a sonic blast that destroyed the fifth planet. Who knows but a sonic wave could have destroyed it. It could have left some pieces bigger and some pieces smaller. If it was a wave power explosion the pieces would be all huge and uneven. Until I study and get a configuration of all the sizes there it is hard for me to really determine what destroyed the planet. What I am trying to ask you to understand is that a sonic wave is another possibility of how the fifth planet was destroyed.

Now I do not know if this is a comeuppance or not but I think that I am correct here and most people might not put these two dots together. The neutron motor or the nuclear motor that we have in our planet Earth could have originally been in the fifth planet. The center of the fifth planet was the neutron or nucleus of a planetary motor and its tanks can be refilled with nuclear energy. The neutrons and protons can be funneled down into this motor to keep it going. Remember how hot this motor was if it was gas and gas burns. Gas has to have oxygen to work. There is no oxygen underneath the dirt that would feed the flame. The nuclear motor heated the fifth planet up so that the planet could be mined separating it and pulling all of the essence out of every crack, corner, and rock in the planet.

The nuclear motor inside the fifth planet went awry and exploded the planet from the inside out. It malfunctioned somehow and it blew the planet apart and all the rocks were scattered from the inside out. This would account for a perfect recognition of why they are all in small pieces from this inside out explosion. This is what you do to an asteroid if it was trying to come down such as Armageddon. That makes logical sense of how it could have been destroyed. So, it could have been a reaction of nuclear type of material.

Now another way the planet could have been destroyed like this into all these little pieces was because of some kind of contamination or disease on the planet. Maybe there was some kind of medical emergency or disease among the inhabitants of the fifth planet. Maybe the water supply became contaminated which caused some type of horrendous disease. They had to destroy the planet in order to eradicate the contamination. In any case is that there was some medical emergency or some medical disease that made the extraterrestrials like they are now.

Another way that the asteroid planet could have been destroyed in a logical manner of connecting the dots was that it was destroyed by the people on Mars who were at war with the people on the fifth planet. It was a war conflict between Mars and the fifth planet. Mars and the fifth planet were in a war of good versus evil. They had a skirmish and then they had to come to planet Earth.

There is no logical reason for the fifth planet to have been destroyed into pieces unless the extraterrestrials who lived there did it. What they are actually telling us is that these two new guys, the Yin and Yang brothers, destroyed their own planet. We are assuming that they destroyed their planet into rocks and pieces during some type of war with each other. I believe it was an ongoing event that the Yin and Yang brothers had because neither one of them wins.

All you need to understand is that there were two warring factions such as the Yin and Yang brothers on the asteroid planet that basically became upset with each other to the point of final frustration the same as two chickens fighting in the barnyard. One evidently had a weapon that caused more destruction than the other one. Since they were two brothers who did not get along, they blew up the planet. Or they made the planet so unstable that it came apart. Either way, the planet was destroyed and they had to move to planet Earth. Did the other people on the asteroid belt planet survive? Did they also come to planet Earth with the Yin and Yang brothers? It is just your way of going to put the pieces together or connecting the dots.

Maybe the Yin and Yang brothers had a fight over the fifth planet's water supply. You never know. This is what is unknown about space. The fight may have been about stealing the satellite that contained the fifth planet's water supply. You never know what the realization is unless somebody shows it to us. But we can theorize. Maybe you can help connect the dots and make it possible to understand.

Okay, ask yourself this if we can even come close to answering this question. Is there another solar system that has a "Goldilocks zone" like we have that has an asteroid belt in it? Do you follow what I am trying to say? Is there another copy of this same scenario someplace else in all the galaxies throughout the space? Now if we do have this reoccurring situation it would lead you to understand that it was intentionally done for some reason or another instead of a warring type of action. The only thing that we do not know is why they went to war or anything about it. It does not really matter but what does matter is that they transcended from there. We do not know if the inhabitants of the asteroid belt basically came with the other people to settle and colonize the planet Earth but it seems that way just because you have the constant Yin and Yang back and forth of terror and hope, black and white, whatever you want to call it. It doesn't matter. It is all the same thing.

Was it a manmade destruction that basically destroyed the fifth planet? Or was it a natural destruction? Or was it finally that the answer to this is that the planet just became too old. It is very simple that when they are done with the planet there they did not need the planet. Okay. They did not need to worry about the orbit that was established when the planet was one solid sphere. So, once they had taken everything that they needed from the fifth planet they broke it all up into little rocks from the inside out and took that motor with them and brought it to planet Earth. Then they heated that motor up and installed it in planet Earth and started all over again. That sounds like good business sense to me about how you would reuse it just like you would reuse space rockets or use that payload over and over again. So here again the logic of business and the logic of existence work together in reconquering another sphere.

But anyway, these are some of the reasons why the fifth planet could be the way it is. You tell me how can you break the planet into all the size rocks there? Then they all stay in the same orbit and have not been shot out everywhere but yet the orbit still remains. This shows you it was either done by destruction or for destruction. Or it was done for a mining situation because the best way to mine a planet is to heat it up from the inside out and get everything that you can from it and what is left is, excuse me for saying, like the dirt clods of the continents. Then they move on to the next planet. This is more likely now that you think about it than the point of them going through a war type of affair. Then again you have the realization of the atomic weapons being detonated on Mars so whichever is correct. Was it a war or was it a domination of who is going to earth next? Whatever it was we do not know the answer to the question.

You have to step back and realize that Earth, Mars, and the asteroid planet are in what you would call the golden zone in our solar system. By that I mean that it is the warmest area of all those or the most tranquil area for our species to live. So, you have Earth, you have Mars, and you have the Asteroid planet and everything else is a little bit too far out and too cold or a little bit too close and too warm.

So, if you will realize the possibility that the fifth planet was destroyed and the people on the fifth planet did not have a place to go. They could not go to Mars because it was too contaminated from the nuclear blast. So, they went to planet Earth because it was the perfect "Goldilocks zone" since it was not too hot or too cold. And if you go traveling or camping what do you have to take with you? The answer is you have to take water. They needed to bring a satellite with them to hold their water.

I bet that satellite that they brought with them could very possibly be the moon that we call the universe all canteen that we have around our planet Earth. It is ironic if you break it down that their coming to planet Earth was like a large camping experience. When everyone left the planet and relocated to another planet that they had to take their water supply with them. And they had to have a container large enough to hold that water supply.

So anyway, after realizing that the moon itself is a satellite I wonder where it came from and why it came to the planet Earth. It came to Earth because it was brought with them to hold the water that they already had. It was already in use on the planet that was destroyed. They just happened to bring it with them and the moon just happened to be hollow. It would be funny if that is what they stored the water in or something of that nature to transport the water.

So here again you have to keep everything in reality in organization to realize that even these guys here after they get done with planet Earth you might never know they might go to another whole solar system completely different and guess what, take the universe all canteen with them to just one more solar system to do over and over again. Would you not carry your canteen with you to do the same thing from solar system to another solar system?

It seems logical to me that in order to verify what might have destroyed the fifth planet you would need to reassemble all of the rocks to see what size planet they would create. It is funny to me is that no one has ever accumulated all of the rocks in the asteroid belt to see what size planet that it would make. In other words reassemble it like it was before it was destroyed. Then with the mass that was created from all the rocks see what kind of orbit and what size of orbit that mass of planet would have. I would like to do the math problem to see what size planet it would create. If you reassembled all the rocks together you would have to have a computer that could allow it to become true. That would be an interesting project.

Then again if you put all of the rocks together so you could do a soil analysis of it to see if it was an aluminum compound. You might find out that our moon is made of the same compound as the planet we call the asteroid belt.

Interesting thought, we also need to find out the total distance of the circumference of the path of the asteroid belt. How long does it go around in the orbit? How long is the path? What is the path of the orbit that it did have? In other words, if the planet was there then how big would it be? From the rocks in the area, what would the circumference around the planet be? What would be the circumference of its orbit? That is an interesting thing. Ask yourself how big is the orbit? How many rocks are in the orbit of the asteroid belt? Now remember the math problem was what size would the planet have been? Here again what I am saying is what was the size of the planet before it became the asteroid belt. And it could possibly have had a satellite around it like a moon.

I could be wrong but if somebody would listen to me then we could put all of the rocks that are in the asteroid belt together to see what size planet they would make. If it was too small then we could add in the moon, the universe all canteen, which was a storage container of water. We do not know all the answers to these questions. So think about the mathematical problem of the original size of the fifth planet this way. If you add together all the rocks in the asteroid belt, the universe all canteen or moon, and the parts on the outside of the universe all canteen then you might know the size of the fifth planet.

What I do not understand is if the fifth planet's rocks are still there why they have not jumbled together and made another planet. The asteroid belt used to be a planet but it was destroyed. Most smart people understand this as it is just how you go down the road. So there again you have to understand why all the rocks are there. So simply just think about trying to come up with a good math problem to come up with a way to go ahead and figure out how many of those rocks are flying around that orbit and then reassemble them if you could by size or mass to see what size planet you could create. There again lies the rub, was it larger than Mars or smaller than Mars? We don't have a picture describing what it was like before it was an asteroid belt. How large was the planet or how small was it? That is the whole key here. If it was a larger planet than Mars, then maybe that would have kept Mars from having a lot of plant life on it or perhaps something of that nature. You never know.

Were there any artifacts that were left on the asteroid belt planet and have they been tested? Until somebody does the math and does the survey of the asteroid planet's debris and reassembles it into the size of the planet that it would be, we have no idea of the size, do we? I think that the size of the asteroid planet was virtually the same size of the planet Earth because it was made to order to fit.

So, if you are on the asteroid planet and you have a war that destroys the planet there should be some residue or some artifacts left. There actually are plenty of them. They just have not been shown to us. The only real way to know if someone was there would be to go out and check the pieces and see if any of the artifactual pieces are from the asteroid belt.

You have heard the saying "as above so below" from Greek mythology and used by astrologers. So therefore, where is the pictorial picture showing us the fifth planet in our solar system? There has to be one somewhere. Where would you go to find such a picture in history's documentation other than some relief picture on a piece of stone or carved on a wall somewhere or painted on a wall? Other than that you are out of luck unless someone gives us a book of history called the Akashic record. There you go. Again, ask yourself maybe the extraterrestrials had the wool pulled over their eyes by their creators. And so the saga goes around and round until there is no answer. There is no answer, there is just perpetuating on and on.

What did the Mayans and the Egyptians use as a sign for the fifth planet when they described how everything was on the land base here on Earth? Did they show you? Did they have established that there was a fifth planet at one time? Because in their way of laying things out on the sand of all on the planet Earth here they allowed for a fifth planet ring to be there, correct? So what did they put in that fifth planet ring and such that we could look back upon in their scribblings in the sand and maybe determine if they drew it as a planet with a satellite? In other words, is there any representation of the fifth planet being shown as a planet with a satellite or moon around it depicted on the face of the earth below? Or do it this way, what did the ancients do to picturize the asteroid belt planet on the face of the earth? Now that is a logical good question and I am sure there is an easy answer for it. But remember with all answers you have to take time to solve it, it is not an overnight game.

The asteroid belt used to be a planet. There is no way around it. You cannot beat the math on this but they do not tell you how it was destroyed. So that leads us to believe the extraterrestrials once lived on the fifth planet but destroyed the planet and then moved away. We do not know how many times they might have done this to planets in the past. This is a curiosity question about the asteroid belt and things of this nature. It makes you wonder when you look at other solar systems out there if there are any other asteroid belts in those solar systems.

So if the fifth planet was not destroyed what would the science project be? What would the magnetic signature of our solar system be if the fifth planet was reengaged and reassembled in size? Then we would know possibly if Earth's satellite, the moon, was originally assembled there, or the moon was a part of the fifth planet. Now this is very logical. And that the little asteroid rocks that are around in the belt might not assemble to be the size of a planet. Now that could very well be. If you take the size of the moon and add it to the dimensional size of all those rocks, would it be the planet that became both of these entities together and they would become the size of the planet?

CHAPTER EIGHT

THE PLANET EARTH

The Goldilocks Zone

We learned in our science classes in school that the planet Earth is the third planet in the solar system and its position is in what is called the "Goldilocks Zone". It is not too close to the sun where it would be too hot and it is not too far away from the sun where it would be too cold. It is just right and where it allows liquid water to exist and provide for life and growth on the planet.

We also learned in our science classes that the Earth rotates on its axis and turns a complete circle every twenty-four hours which creates daytime and nighttime. As the Earth rotates it also orbits around the sun in an elliptical path which takes three hundred sixty-five days or one year. The Earth is also tilted twenty-three degrees on its axis. The four seasons are caused by the tilt of the Earth's axis away from or toward the sun as it travels through its orbit around the sun.

The Earth also wobbles on its axis as it spins like a gyroscope or top. Just like a top as it winds down the Earth wobbles towards the sun and away from the sun. This wobble which is called the precession takes twenty-six thousand years to complete a full three hundred sixty degree cycle or one degree every seventy two years. These motions of the Earth change how much light and energy each hemisphere receives from the sun during the orbit around the sun, when the seasons occur, and how extreme the seasonal changes are.

It has been said that a meteor or asteroid supposedly hit the planet Earth and knocked off the outer crust and these rocks went around and around in a circle and created the moon. Okay, so what happened to the thing that hit the Earth? Well, it is said that it supposedly went inside the Earth. Okay, now how mathematically illogical is it to have something that goes inside the Earth but not destroy it? In other words, what they are actually telling us is that these new guys, extraterrestrials or the Yin and Yang brothers, destroyed their planet into rocks and pieces.

All right, then what was it that went inside the earth? Was it metal or something of that nature? Or was it gas? This cannot be true because if it was just gas then somebody would hit a pocket and it would empty out like a tire deflating in the atmosphere wouldn't it? There would be no control over it. What we are saying here is what? They put something inside of the planet Earth and it created Earth into turning. It is almost like if you can understand a percolator, a coffee pot, that you put a lightbulb in the center of the balloon and turn it on. Does the balloon expand with heat as it heats up?

Of course, I believe that the earth has a geothermal center engine in it that they inserted into the planet to create the planet to grow the planet like it is because if you have heat inside you can grow everything from the inside out. There again you just realize having the point of view of having a warm planet and that it looks blue in the night sky from the moon.

So, if you think about the earth being a blue ball in the sky from space, why is it blue? It is blue because there is a little heater motor inside allowing the water to have reflective capabilities because of the heat transferring through the water coming to the surface. Why is it a blue ball and not a black ball? Okay, so it has to have some lighting effects somewhere so it has to have energy.

So how do you get a nuclear motor inside of another planet? Well the Bible said that God took seven days to create Earth. Right? What we are talking about is that we are trying to heat up the planet by putting a lightbulb inside of it or whatever to keep the planet perking. If the planet did not have a heat type of style motor remember that we would not have life because the essence of heat is life. Without heat nothing goes on. You do not have expansion of cells. You do not have this and you do not have that. So without heat you basically have nothing.

What we are saying here is what? They put something inside of the planet Earth that creates Earth into turning. It is almost like if you can understand a percolator or a coffee pot that you put a lightbulb in the center of the balloon and turn it on. Does the balloon expand with heat as it heats up? Of course it does. Well remember how hot is this motor if it was gas and gas burns. Gas has to have oxygen to work and this is inside of the planet. So there is no oxygen underneath the dirt that would feed the flame. So, it has to be a reaction of nuclear type of material.

So they, the extraterrestrials or the Yin and Yang brothers, had to insert a neutron motor or an atomic motor inside the planet Earth to basically heat the planet up so they can live here. Remember we are in space and it is cold so you have got to have heat. So how cold is the floor where you live when you put your feet on it? Then you deal with the possibility that the extraterrestrials heated the planet Earth up for seven days so they could install this neutron or electron or nuclear motor inside of it. Then everything else cools down around it because it is so hot that it has to be cooled. So this would tell us that there is no water on it at this time, correct? So basically how do you cool down a nuclear motor or an atomic motor? With water because water turns into steam in the atmosphere and comes back down and stays.

Where did this water that was used to cool the Earth come from? There was no water on the planet. The extraterrestrials brought the water with them in the moon, the universe all canteen. You have to have water. Water was used to cool the Earth after it was heated up. Water was needed for life. Plants and animals and everything need water. Water was needed to terraform the Earth. Water was needed in the oceans, rivers, and lakes for marine life. Water was needed to complete the environmental transformation from one planet to another.

Maybe the extraterrestrials brought the moon with them to our planet here to be an accompaniment planet from Mars and the asteroid belt that was destroyed. They came here to Earth and brought the moon with them. When they brought their stuff here they made the moon basically a secondary planet. Imagine that the people are still living inside Mars there. It is an interesting concept and both civilizations are living together. But the point of view of what we are saying is the reason you carry your water with you if you had destroyed the planet where you lived and moved to another planet is you have to have water in order to live. It is what you have to have when in space and traveling to the earth.

There have been reports of extraterrestrials hanging over nuclear power plants. They are hanging over these large energy wave manufacturing things. It is sort of amazing that they always go for energy waves to make it all work. There has to be an energy somehow that keeps it going on planet Earth. They are trying to keep the planet alive, right? How many times do they have to come down here to the planet and put more fuel into the engine if they did not correctly do the math to where it has to be serviced? In other words, does the engine that we have in our planet, does it have to be serviced and have new energy put in it so we can continually do the mining operation and allow life to exist on the planet? Now there you go. Not a bad idea.

When Admiral Byrd flew over Antarctica, he noticed an orifice type entryway going down into the base of the earth that was a nice and smooth entryway that was like the opening of a carburetor. This carburetor type opening is the same type of entryway in the earth. You know, think of the extraterrestrials having an opening to go down into the base of the mountain. Imagine the same type of opening posted all over the planets that we associate with. This also tells that the extraterrestrials could live inside the planet. So therefore, if I was an extraterrestrial where would I go? Well evidently where you cannot find me, right?

If the extraterrestrials can live inside the planet then they can grow their crops inside the planet in a controlled environment area. Now did you listen to what I just said? If they grow them inside a controlled environment area, you do not need the "real sun" or anything like it to grow your food. You could basically create your own space time dimension and everything else by making it a dome facility enclosure encapsulation. So basically, we can grow food twenty-four hours a day and seven days a week not only on top of the earth or when the sun is exposed. When you control the sun and the elements you control when it grows and when it blooms. This is the same thing with us, right?

Why did they come here? The extraterrestrials came to live here on planet Earth so they could mine it because it had water or they brought water with them whatever the case may be. Did they destroy the planet where they came from and then came to Earth? We do not know but we do know that they have the ability to travel from planet to planet probably to harvest the planet for what they need. Think of how many different types of planetary harvest stations could be there and each extraterrestrial group could have their own solar system to go through and plunder.

Maybe the only real realization that we have not talked about is they came here to extrapolate the minerals out of the planet. Okay, so ask yourself the question after they get all the stuff out of our planet, squeeze out all the oil, all the fracking, all the gasoline, all this and all that and there is nothing left for them to live for or to be here with or to take from the planet or that they need to ingest or whatever they do with it, then would you not just basically travel on to the next closest planet yourself? And there again start all over again the process. Therefore taking a dead rock and put something inside that heats it up to see what comes out through the pores in the skin or as we call it, the earth which is nothing more than the magma sneaking through the gaps in the door allowing the inside to puddle up in the snow or basically expose the remnants that are within and once it heats up it is like a pot of water on the stove. What do you get after you boil it up? So, imagine how much heat you have to have to keep the center of the earth hot with all these volcanoes with lava for these billions of years? It could not be gas. It has to be atomic energy. So, ask yourself the question, did they insert it into the planet earth? Yes, they did.

It makes you wonder where did the essence all come from if the extraterrestrials put in a large electronic pulse figure that they had to create because when they ignited this bomb and it exploded that it started heating and swirling these things in there. On planet Earth they are controlling the heat process as a thermal nuclear reactor and keeping it cool with the waters from the oceans.

As the planet cools and does its thing then the miners come in and do the process from one end to the other on the planets that they desire to mine. I guess you have to really understand that the planet has its own basically primary signature of the elements that are on it by its periodic table of elements. So the planet would have to be studied and tested to see what it would have on it plus if it has the right things on it then you can basically send a biological spray of acids and oozes and stuff until you get there and take advantage of what had already been created thousands of years before earlier than you so when you get there you have control over them. That might be a different way to look at things.

If we are not educated then ninety-nine percent of us will never understand that the planet Earth could be nothing more than a huge mining colony facility that provides goods for everybody else in the rest of the solar system as well as other dimensions. We transcend and maybe that is when we have a chance to go to the next Promised Land as it is called reality. When you break everything down to the basics then you start to realizing and understanding the essence of life, cosmic consciousness, and things of that nature. When you learn to treat everything with equal respect is when you rise above the spooze of humanity and really become a human instead of an uneducated individual.

Planet Earth is the world's largest mining adventure. Look at what they are doing here on our planet and just think about the planet is nothing more than a large mining project. They are harvesting all of the chemicals and minerals from inside the planet. The planet was created with all of its minerals to be a huge mining project.

Think about the gold rush decades ago with all the gold mixed in with the dirt in the bottoms of streams. Now the question is very simple. How can you find gold saturated in such a large area such as these mining projects but only get little specks of gold? There is no way that these little specks of gold could be from a single report. It had to be put in when it was in a flash process. In other words, it was not in a solid form. Because these little specks of gold were mixed in with the dirt it would indicate that it was from a coronal mass ejection spray when the Earth was created that allowed the Earth to be saturated in certain places more than others. This was probably caused by the positioning of the planet when it was being exposed to the disruption of the coronal mass ejection from the sun.

People are always looking for this gold or silver. Now ask yourself an easy question. Where would this come from? Why would you want to scatter it all over the planet? How can it be spread throughout the entire planet? When the planet Earth was created it was nothing more than a discharge from the sun. Not knowing what is inside is why all the excavator spacemen most likely are doing an inventory of what is in the planet. Once they realized the planet was good they heated it up with the motor in it and brought the water back to cool it off so they could most likely control the heat separation so they could mine it.

If they are mining the planet of all the chemicals and minerals, then think about all the other minerals in the periodic table of elements we are looking for that are not in a certain solid point in what you call a pure strike. We get saturated with little specks and pieces scattered everywhere. Not until the Earth started to cool did we realize how deep in the earth the gold was. How deep are they going to dig it out? Most people just cannot see the logic of dissolving the gold from within instead of digging it out. That is the way to go and mine from the inside out and not from the outside in.

The only way to mine anything is to completely dissolve it and see what is inside. If you sit back and think about it they could actually be controlling the dissolving of the planet under our feet through a large global mining process of a solar mining process that we are completely oblivious to.

You keep hearing me say to mine the planet Earth. Now in your world you think that mining is going from the outside going down, correct. I understand that is correct in your way of thinking but in my way of thinking you mine from the inside where it is hottest going to the surface. You get only tidbits and I get all the good stuff that is deep inside. In other words the good gold is always deep in the planet. Why dig down with your hands when you can dissolve it with water from within. That is the way to go from the inside out and not from the outside in.

Remember the essence. I guarantee you the warmer it is the easier it is to extract what you are extracting.

When you mine and have mining construction and debris you want to create slaves or workers to go ahead and take care of the mining and do all the lifting and all the toting. Then the people that are the workers become your science project.

You have to understand the pressure zones to create the planet out of nothing more than just charcoal and dust. That is just the way it is. It is just a way of purifying the materials out of it through a heat process. How did the extraterrestrials learn how to get together all the raw elements it takes to put inside of the sun? Now just understand this to put the elements inside the sun and then activate it where it starts the process of reducing itself down into a more solid essence base which we call the vein of gold or silver. There again making the planets and then mining the planets. You have to understand how the planets are created before you understand how to mine the planets.

Now do we understand the hollow earth and how the mining takes place? The people on the bottom do not know what the people on the top are doing because there is too much land mass in the middle. Also, the extraterrestrials know how to keep us at bay by not letting us see their points of entry or exit. So, we are dealing with a hollow earth effect by mining from the inside out. Most people mine from the outside going in because it is all they know, everything from the essence outside going in. But I am trying to tell you if you understand the essence like I do from the inside going out then you cannot confuse me.

It is just hard to understand that the planet Earth and all these other planets might be nothing more than a mining exploration conquest. Then when you are done with this mining complex you have got to move your machinery to the next site. I think I am correct with the world mining situation and all. I am trying to say here that the periodic table of elements and everything that is in it that I do not think you know how to apply the table in the correct applications to create the different things that I am being brought to explain and show to you even though it is not going to be visible in your books to see and understand it. You have to go with the faith and understanding and the logic until we go through the process of trying it and seeing the yield of our thoughts and decisions. Here you will not know the true outcome and if I am allowed to be a part of it then you will have the original essence from the inside out instead of trying to reverse engineer it from the outside in. That is all I can try to give you my friends. If you will not listen then I am not going to force it on you.

The planet Earth is made of land masses or continents and bodies of water or oceans. Why don't the continents on the planet Earth dissolve into the water? The continents have a layer of dirt and dirt dissolves into water. Now listen to me again to what I am saying. Why don't the continents dissolve? It is just too obvious that there is some kind of barrier or magnetic wave between the continents and the water to keep the planet intact. But yet they try to split the continents up into slices and pieces and allow them to go in the water so they can remove the stuff inside them. This is an interesting point of view. They use the water to destroy the continents but water does not dissolve the continents. Water can split the continents through heat and freezing and stuff like that in fracking and cracking and impacting craters and aquifers but the continents do not ever dissolve into the water even after billions of years. There has to be a ring of protection around the planet Earth. It is like there is an underwater sea area creating a magnetic ring that basically shields the water from having a chance to atomize or liquefy the dirt in my opinion.

I still think that the Earth's core motor discharges its heat wave hot water into the ocean causing the heated water that comes up by Africa to create those hurricanes and storms. It is not all the time and there might be a different place to put the hot water but I do not know. I just do not understand taking hot water all of a sudden from one place and putting it in another place that is thousands of miles away from where the water got hot and yet the water is the same temperature. There was just too much mass of all the water that has not been heated up to make that transfer. What I can understand is the British thermal unit element type of stuff. There again I am just trying to answer the question of why do you always have heat and water hotter in an area where supposedly the heat was brought from a current that allows it to go around in the ocean, right? What makes that current move? Heat, right. There again answer the question if heat makes things move it then it makes light and everything.

Maybe this time they stopped themselves before they totally destroyed the planet. In other words, they might have caught themselves from destroying the planet Earth here like they had had done before on the other planet. In other words, they might have realized all the problems that caused them to explode the asteroid belt planet. Maybe this time they stopped themselves from total obliteration again on planet Earth and that is what they are doing here now. They destroyed the asteroid planet. Here again the same Yin and Yang brothers might have been close to doing the same thing here. Who knows, maybe they achieved their goal and maybe they did not. Maybe it is a science project that they are trying to figure out as it goes on and on until we get there. Maybe they have nothing else to do or it is test question they have to ask. We don't know because we are not there yet.

Remember why was the planet Earth left empty of all the different people of all the different civilizations? All of a sudden there is nobody on the planet Earth at all. Nobody is here and it is an empty place and we are going to have to start all over again with the history of everything else. Now that sounds sort of strange. There are always remains of these civilizations of the past and the only thing that remains is these stones. It makes you wonder what really happened here. Could it have been a medical emergency that contaminated the whole planet here on planet Earth and they had to kill off all the people? We do not know. Just think about it like that. And here again think about in another touch of extraterrestrial stuff here. Did they not possibly do what they did on the asteroid planet, except with that situation they destroyed the planet to get rid of it or cleansed it or whatever the case may be? Did they almost do the same thing again on the planet Earth that they did on the asteroid planet and that they might have done the same mistake again? This only means one or two different things. They are trying to go about a scientific problem the same way they did it before and made a mistake except this time they just killed the people on the planet. Or is this time a totally new type of situation and we go down the road? I do not know. Just think about it logically if it was not for a science experiment that totally would have annihilated or eliminated everybody from the planet Earth, nothing physical, nothing visible, and nothing else for what other reason would everybody be removed from the planet Earth. Let's say everybody was removed to go ahead and populate someplace else. Okay fine, and then again you have the possibility of that actually this is nothing more than this is a huge farm of life and that all of the humans that were here are being taken away for different types of food to be put on the extraterrestrials' menu.

The question that I am asking you to understand is where did all the people go that enabled us to start the whole civilization deal all over again? That is sort of funny. You have all the stuff that says what our future is that now that we are starting to understand it. So what makes you think if has not happened ten times or one hundred times before until we really understand and get off the Petri dish and get a chance to get up in the stars and see and become one of the all-knowing people instead of children of the galaxy. We are just food for thought and all we think about is things that could have been the question. You have to remember in your own self is that if they made us in their image and they got to do the same things we do they eventually will think with a different ability because they are older and have a different technology but that basic essences have always been the same. They have to eat, they have to sleep, they have to poop and they are always wondering the most key thing of all which is where did they come from.

You know, it all starts to make sense. We always wondered how all the people who were on the planet disappeared. What happened here on the planet Earth is nothing more than a simple science experiment that wiped out everybody that was here. The ones that did survive are the ones that repopulated the planet as such. Where did the people go that were here before? Was it a disease? How can a disease wipe out all of the people? There is no evidence. Maybe that is why the extraterrestrials are the way they are. Maybe this was a bad science experiment that went awry and contaminated the gene pool on the planet Earth. But when you have a total gene pool population extinction with nobody left over it has to have been a disease because it was a bad science experiment. Unless they took the whole population but that doesn't make any sense of taking the entire population unless the reason you would take an entire population is for the simple reason you can start anew with a different agenda or refined agenda. Why would you take an entire population if you could start a new or different or better or refined agenda? It had to be a medical malfunction. That is the only thing that can be a logical explanation. Either that or we are just a large food source for them to eat and they came here and harvested us the same as we harvest the animals that we eat. We are just animals. Slow down, it is just the same answers. The same essence answers that take place in the future are the same thing that happens now. The only difference between now and then are the faces on the people.

Just remember one simple thing. The God that I know and that I represent created the essence of all this dimension is made of. That is right, the creation made the essence possible that brought forth to us to have the essence to manipulate so we could create; therefore, thinking we are something great. But we are nothing for using tools that were left over from somebody once before. So here again you know you just have to understand the whole point of view of where is it enough. Why is everybody whitewashed in their mind from stopping to ask these different questions? How many times do you have to see the faces have been re-modified and changed to represent something different?

Okay, remember according to the Bible it took seven days to create the heavens and the Earth. Now according to the Bible God created the heavens and the Earth. The Bible said that it had no shape or form. Right? Well it had some kind of shape because it was a rock but when water was put on the Earth that made it round. Basically, he created the essence first. Then he went back and turned what we call Earth into a viable planet. So therefore, when we say that it took seven days to create the heavens and the Earth what we are really saying is that took seven days in my opinion to basically heat the planet up into a formable shape that would accept a nuclear motor. Look at it this way as a junior size sun that we could put inside of the planet to go ahead and further the space mining exploration conquest. Here we go again it connects the dots. That is just what we do.

All we are simply saying here is that in the point of view of the Earth having the motor stuck inside of it and taking seven days to create so it would allow the other little junior suns as I call them to be installed inside a solid planet or a solid rock form that would support human life as such. So it was heated and molded as was mentioned earlier.

Now let's address the possibility that it is really too hot. So how do you cool down a molten rock in space especially if you are terraforming it? Well logically in my world as I see it I would basically say we had to put water on the face of the Earth so we could basically cool the planet down and start the Earth mining project just like they did on all the other planets in all the other solar systems. That is my projection of why the planets are a storage facility of all the raw materials that were put in them. You heard it here first folks. That is right. That is what I am saying. What do you think about that logically? What do you think about the planet Earth, okay?

CHAPTER NINE

THE UNIVERSE ALL CANTEEN

The Moon

This chapter is the arrival of the extraterrestrials to our planet therefore starting off the whole point of view of the universal canteen or as I call it "The Universe All Canteen". Now this has only to do with the planet Earth and how it all relates to it and I will be able to explain the universe all canteen to you. So basically here we go. You have to relax and open your mind up to realize that what you are going to hear is a very logical possibility. It only starts to answer the questions in which we have no end to but it just gives us hope that one day we will be able to finalize and make an overall picture and get off the petri dish and to analyze what most do not have the time to analyze and understand. This is what I am doing. I am showing you the other view of the petri dish that most people do not have the time to understand or learn and become.

Here we go. Imagine that you are all powerful and that you are the Yin and Yang brothers, the two elements that are in this dimension and everything. The point of the universe all canteen comes into our view by the moon being towed into place or all of a sudden appearing. There is not a moon and then one day all of a sudden there is a moon. The point of this arrival type of situation is basically the point of view of when they came here and evolved here to be able to live on planet Earth and all they have to do is what?

Well, if you imagine that if you went camping or that you are moving a whole society from one planet to another whole new planet, what is the most important thing that you would need if you were made in our image? Well if they are made in our image then they have to have the same things that we do. You have to have water, food, sunlight, and oxygen to go have its basic construction to go down the road.

So here again with the universe all canteen and how does this all start off and how does this all take place? What does all this mean to us since everybody is clueless? Shall we start the process? The process with the universe all canteen is very simple to understand. If you went camping, how much water would you carry if you are going a month into the desert? Well, you are going to carry all that you can or all that you are going to need because water is the most precious of all, correct? Water, food, oxygen, air. Okay, so once these items are known and that is what they have to have to grow and they have to have them on the planet then they would have to terraform the planet of some nature to allow themselves to have and establish a base here or another colony as they are doing and coming this way. So as the universe all canteen is in space as you all now call it the moon realize one simple thing that if you are warring factions, you are the Yin and Yang brothers, they can never win you can never lose so why would you play the game is the answer to all this book.

Therefore, you have to realize that there was no water on the planet Earth until they brought the water with them in the universe all canteen. The reason we call it the universe all canteen is how could you bring so much water with you if you destroyed your planet and had to move to a new planet? How could you bring the water? You are going to have to have a place to pour it into and leave it in reserve in the moon up above. Interesting huh? So as we go down the road the point of all is a universe all canteen.

So, getting back to understanding that the universe all canteen is a man-made moon. It is the universal eye or the all-seeing eye as you would call it so they can monitor us and keep track of us and keep track of those on the planet as we grow on

Earth. When the moon was towed into place it sure is mathematically possible and probable for it to be the exact same size of this for it to work out. It is mathematically perfect so you would be able to look up and wonder about the stars, of why the sky went black and then came light again. Think of the knowledge and of happening of something got in between. It is like a lightbulb went off that it is there. In other words you were basically shown that there was movement in the stars that was not seen before. If you were still going on this camping trip that we talked about basically you have to understand the point of view that if you go camping or traveling someplace you have to take all your supplies with you such as if we were to go back to Mars.

So realizing that we used to live on Mars and given the point that there is nuclear residue left on the planet Mars it leads you to only one simple conclusion that the overall picture of all the planets used to be all together in one form. In other words, the asteroid belt used to be a planet but something happened where it was destroyed. So imagine and just understand the point of view that Mars and we are going to call it the asteroid planet actually had people living on them. They were our fathers and they are warring factions, the two Yin and Yang brothers, and because of their non-complacency they did not want to get along with each other such as the Democrats and Republicans in the United States today. Look at what they do to themselves and look at how they beat themselves up and tear themselves down. These two Yin and Yang brothers who can never win one way or the other, right? One day they will realize to not play the game.

But the point of view of the universe all canteen is to go ahead and realize how all it ever came to be on our planet. Well, you have to realize and understand these two warring brothers basically are the Yin and Yang brothers that we are talking about. So basically, everything in the area where they lived was destroyed. So if you logically just allow yourself to absorb what is in front of your eyes is how can you have all these planets in our solar system, these perfectly formed planets and then have this bunch of little rocks that didn't congeal together with all the others. It makes no logical concession that these planets would not have been some kind of ball put together like with all the others. What does make perfect logical sense is that the planet was busted up into pieces from some type of a sonic device.

But in any case, the universe all canteen was moved into place. Remember these two warring factions have just destroyed their planet from years of warring just like they are doing here on the planet Earth. So basically, you have to ask yourself when they finally figured out how they destroyed their planet they had to have a place to go, didn't they? They have to take all the water with them that they could, all the food that they could, and everything else they would need to come this way. It was almost like an ark that came this way to bring everything towards this other area that they had destroyed and had done before. And here again we are only assuming that they destroyed that other planet. As far as we know they might have basically removed all the minerals and everything and terraformed it to where they wanted to leave it. Only when they left it they destroyed the planet so nobody else can get anything out of it or whatever their real reason to leave the planet in that way.

But here again now that you understand you have to have water and you have to move if you destroyed the planet where you lived and radiation is your enemy. Well you would have to leave that area and go someplace else. Earth is the next logical spot to stop and start the same situation from planet to planet over and over again. It is not that hard to understand but what is difficult for most people is to realize that you have the power to destroy the whole planet through sonic vibrations of whichever way that allowed all this to take place which allowed them to come to our planet here.

But back to the universe all canteen that we were talking about and the water that they brought with them. Just imagine that if you did this to your planet or your area and you have to transfer and come to the planet Earth and transform it into what you are doing. It makes only more logical sense if you understand that the moon is full of water and you had to have a place that it would be a logical place to terraform the planet Earth.

Now here again you think that the planet Earth is round because that is how you see it. Imagine the planet Earth before we put water on it and before we developed it. It was just a blob out in the middle but then they inserted the electronic or nuclear motor into it. Then they put the water on the planet here as a three part process. First, the water on the planet cools the energy that is radiating from within. Second, the water is put here as a counterbalance to keep it all in balance and spinning. Third, the water is needed by the extraterrestrials since they have started colonizing this planet and changing all the wildlife that was brought to this planet so they can start over.

How else would you transport and transfer an entire ecosystem to a new home planet? The universe all canteen has everything that is needed to produce a complete new life and ecosystem that could eventually populate the land with all the different variations of DNA. It is an endless supply of life that you can create and direct just like a science project. The universe all canteen has an entire universe within it. It then becomes the universe for all canteen because it is a sphere containing water and a complete ecosystem for transferring and transforming a new planet.

How was all of the marine life brought to planet Earth? The moon which is a hollow satellite could have been used to transport all of the marine life and its ecosystem to the planet. The universe all canteen became the universe for all canteen and transporter because it had all the marine life that had ever probably been created and then contained here on planet Earth. Originally it could have been transported from Mars or the asteroid belt planet when they were destroyed so the marine life was removed from there to planet Earth. They knew the planet was going to be destroyed and doomed so they saved their marine life and its ecosystem by putting them inside the universe for all canteen or what we know as the satellite called the moon. Then they transported it here for a continuation of the same cycle. If we already had water here on the planet then they just added that ecosystem to the water that was here already which maybe was transported already in an earlier shipment that we do not know about. It could have taken two or three times. We have no idea how many times or how many trucks it takes to move a civilization from a planet to another planet much less the ecosystem. So this is just a starting situation or reality instead of what we assume is reality.

Here again is the situation and understanding that the universe all canteen now is a space station and always has been. It is the all-seeing eye. It also controls the weather and the tides and stuff. Just imagine how easy it would be for the people who are in control of the moon to basically all of a sudden say, hey wait a minute we do not like these guys so we are just going to have the flood turn this way or that way and basically wipe them all out and start all over again.

But with the universe all canteen and the water now we realize that the moon itself can also be a positive or negative force or pole that can actually increase the gravity on the planet or decrease the gravity on the planet. As well as they can have a sonic noise or a beacon that keeps all humans in control or basically keeps our brains from being able to think at one hundred percent efficiency which they are designed to do out of the gate. I don't think our mind has to develop but if it does have to develop then that is great. Just imagine that if the other percentage of your mind was kept at check because of a sonic wave thing you called gravity allowed us not to have the upper end thinking that we desire to have only through the point of purging ourselves and being able to oscillate the signal. In other words make ourselves become thinkers to understand yoga and disciplines and to be able to. Why is this happening to us and do you ever know that the signal exists?

The universe all canteen shows us that the possibility of life leads to all of these other parameters. Now remember water on the planet does several different things. It gives us water that we drink and eat and do. It gives us water in the atmosphere which we breathe the oxygen. It gives us water in which the extraterrestrials can live and stay and hide. It gives all the food and stuff we grow in the water that we need to eat and everything. It gives water to help jump start the bio-marine transformation of the planet. So you have to bring water with you if you are our consistency and want to take over a planet or therefore making it terraformed or make it good for your style of being as you are.

I never did the math to find out how many gallons of water the moon could hold inside itself. Also, how much area on the planet Earth would this much water cover up? If this amount of water does not seem like much in comparison to our oceans, then simply understand that to help terraform a planet it helps to have a base to start a weather system on the planet in order to establish the four seasons, correct? The travelers always go prepared when and if they move again when they are done harvesting our planet from all the oil and natural energies that they want they will simply migrate to the next planet and start all over again. If something works why would you ever change that system? There is no telling how many times that this has taken place in the total universe.

So here again with the universe all canteen or the moon and everything being all that I have told now is it not logical that if we are a magnetic thing here and we have all these lay lines that are going around the planet that are already mapped that they are harnessing for the electricity to keep it in our atmosphere here and believe it or not I think that the gravity might actually have something to do with it. I do not know everything but I just know what I know.

Well here let me give you the whole idea of why I thought that the moon was a canteen. At one time I was a Boy Scout and we go camping and we do all these things. So how did I know that the moon was the universe all canteen up there? Well when camping one time in the Boy Scouts we have our canteens. They were an aluminum green thing with a strap. One time I was kneeling down to fill my canteen with water because you are thirsty and my canteen hit a rock and it rang. When I remembered that happening it got me to connect the dots to believe that the moon is nothing more than a universe all canteen.

What started me on this chapter was watching a television program tell about the astronauts landing on the moon. Wernher von Braun, one of the German scientists brought over in Operation Paperclip, and his staff basically were the ones who designed the rockets. The point of view of this was knowing that von Braun had more information about rockets than we did. Von Braun wrote in an article of a March 1970 issue of *Popular Science* magazine that when the Apollo 12 crashed the empty ascent stage of the lunar module on the moon surface that the moon rang like a bell for nearly an hour afterwards. Von Braun could have told the astronauts to go ahead and release that empty fuel cell and let it drop back to the moon just to see what would happen. According to another article in the May 27, 2016 issue of *Popular Science*, the same thing happened on Apollo 13 with the vibrations lasting even longer. This started my reality zone of the moon's vibrational ring. How can the moon ring unless it is a metal canteen? Well ringing means metal like a canteen.

Scientists have projected that the moon is an aluminum alloy. I just wonder if this huge round sphere is being used as a communication point as well as sending signal blocking waves that keep us from using the upper extremities of our brain. Ask yourself, why would they do this? It is for planetary control. We are just science projects.

Remember that Isaac Newton never knew that the moon was made of an aluminum compound. He was never privy to that information. He could not see that. If he knew that he would have understood gravity even more. Most people today do not even realize it. But here again in a bounce effect the moon has to be hollow too because it was towed in place.

If you really realize it when you look at the size of the moon you see that it is perfectly sized and everything. What we are saying here though is that the moon is almost as if it is like a golf ball in the sky. I will give you the reasoning. If you look at the moon you understand that all the impact craters on it seem to have a very limited amount of depth to them. The craters seem to be even sized like the dimples on a golf ball. If you look down at the planet Earth you look at how deep all of those impact craters are. How can the moon not have a huge impact crater a mile deep like we have on our own planet Earth? It makes no logical sense that the moon doesn't have any depth to its impact craters. They are wider and shallower and they are spread out over a larger area over the face of it. The moon is not a dirt planet but a metal planet going into it because of how the depth shows us.

Now this is a scary thing to realize I understand but once you realize that the moon is a universe all metal canteen that held the water that they brought here then it opens up to the other points of view that you have not seen that the moon is also the space station that they control everything with. No wonder we have not had any impact craters on our planet recently because they are simply stopping them from happening. They have the ability to control all this stuff and we do not know it.

And here again why do you think that the moon does not turn around and around to show us what is on the back hand side? What a perfect place to have your base inside the moon on the back hand side where no one could see. They can come and go and do what they want to do. It makes no logical sense of why the moon does not have a large impact crater three quarters of a mile deep. No one is going to do research on the depth of the impact craters on the moon I guarantee.

Now we are very interested in Mars and we recently sent one or two rovers to Mars. There have been shown that there really are ancient buildings on Mars that we all knew was there. What I am trying to say is wouldn't it be neat when we got back to Mars that they made another universe all canteen for the moon. This universe all canteen would be a place where they stored their stuff in case they had to get away as their emergency service get away spaceship. Actually wouldn't that be great to have the universe all canteen as what I call their emergency spaceship in case they have to leave and orbit? Instead of being a satellite around the planet they just take the satellite and putter off. That would be a nice way to go wouldn't it? Always something new.

Maybe this might open you up to the universe all canteen, for the realization that yes they are there. It is the all-seeing eye and it is all a matter of the extraterrestrials controlling us from the beginning to the end. And then being trapped here because of their sin and then evidently not allowing them to go home until they educate us until we become educated like they are. That was the original sin to change us from naturally developing in our own natural form hopefully like they did. So here again if they are our gods then who were their gods? It still pursues on in a never ending thing.

CHAPTER TEN

THE 2012 ANOMALY

December 21, 2012

There never was an answer as to why December 21, 2012 was not the destructive event that had been predicted to take place. It was called a Doomsday Prophecy. December 21, 2012 was a date that was supposed to change the world as we knew it. It was supposed to happen. The ancient Mayans' calendar stopped on December 21, 2012 and many believed that this meant that the world would end on that date. This was the date for the alignment that took place every twenty-six thousand years. It had happened in the past and it was supposed to happen again on December 21, 2012.

There was a media build up detailing that this would be such a monumental and even destructive day. Books, movies, television programs, documentaries, videos, and internet websites all detailed the chaos and destruction that would occur on this date. It was a Doomsday Prophecy. It was supposed to happen. People had been talking about it for decades.

But December 21, 2012 came and nothing happened that we could see or hear. The Earth was not destroyed and there was no devastation as predicted. It was just another day here on planet Earth as far as we know.

Why didn't any of these predicted and highly believed things happen? Why did everybody say that chaos and devastation would take place and it did not? There were records of such happening in the past. Why hasn't anyone given a reason as to why the devastation did not take place on December 21, 2012?

I guess you would say what started my awareness about the 2012 event was learning about the predictions by Nostradamus and others from programs on television. Everything seemed to be focusing towards this monumental point in time through thousands of years of study. It had to be twenty-six thousand years for one complete cycle to throw everything out of kilter as they say as a signatory twenty degrees wobble or such that actually creates the seasons. For some reason I believe that Nostradamus, the Mayans and others predicted the 2012 alignment was because it reoccurred every twenty-six thousand years. Whatever it was kept it from happening this time like it had in the past.

But here again with the situation of what you had with the preparation for 2012 being so dramatic, when it came the time for it to happen that it did not. Nobody has said anything about why it did not happen the way all the Mayans and others such as Nostradamus, Leonardo da Vinci, Edgar Casey, and Isaac Newton predicted. You have all these people like the Mayan legacy and all the codices that they were describing about how bad 2012 was going to be. But nobody came up with an answer as to why it didn't happen. Even the recent ones who predicted that it was going to be a bad day had nothing to say. Nobody even said "oops, we made a mistake, we were wrong". Nobody said anything. There was only silence.

When the December 21, 2012 predicted destruction did not happen it upset me so severely that I wrote this book and had to dig deeper and deeper to find out just what happened. That started my questions of asking and answering my own self through transcendental meditation and astral projection to try to get to the truth. Just go for the truth and see if you can understand the main point of understanding of why it still exists out there. I was able to pick up on the vibrations and time seems to be a logical and timely connecting of the dots in this. It seems to me as if I went all the way to the end of the tunnel and stopped and saw the essence and learned from the essence back out to conscious reality. This is what enables me to be able to flip and flop and do the one hundred eighty different positive degrees that I think with to come up with these possible scenarios.

This all started with why 2012 did not happen and why everybody was wrong for saying that it would happen like it had in the past. If the Mayans knew to study 2012 with the twenty-six thousand years cycle before it actually happened, then it had to have happened before in the past because they started writing it down so they could remember it to tell about it to people on the planet.

There is so much here to this 2012 thing and its answers and these parameters that we do not even understand. How can you have such a magnificent thing like the 2012 event that this did not happen as predicted? There has to be a logical reason why the 2012 event did not take place.

I am beginning to look at 2012 as if it were actually a time, an electrical time lock kind of thing that kept from destroying the Earth as it had all these other times before. The alignment came up every twenty-six thousand years so it would naturally destroy the Earth. Therefore, Satan would have to start over again and start rebuilding his team of warriors to try to force the conclusion of Armageddon at Megiddo. To me this sounds like the 2012 thing was a time lock that went wrong and Satan actually had a chance this last time at 2012 to stop the earth from being destroyed. So therefore, his sin and evil can grow through the internet and things like this which has just amplified everything through the roof.

I believe that the extraterrestrials themselves had a way figured out to finally stop the electrical demise of what was supposed to happen in 2012. Therefore, it would forward their point of view or their agenda as far as the demon type of agenda. Look at it this way as if the extraterrestrials are the Yin and Yang brothers who are actually good versus evil or God versus Satan. Just imagine that if everything was torn up, all right, then how much it would set the whole world back in a torn up situation or a distraction.

I believe it was a positive thing that the extraterrestrials stopped the 2012 event from happening so this would basically help Satan's agenda to stay on time with what is going on today. Think of it this way. It you have evil set back then everybody might actually learn to live together. But because 2012 did not happen so that the devil has his reign and therefore pumping everybody up in a more higher rage than normal. Being that terrorism is the new game in the world with more monetary government and more terrorism that it seems to be the new world order. Doesn't it?

So if that is the case, just think about if 2012 did happen with the destruction. Think about all of the advances and achievements that would have been destroyed. Nothing would be the same. Think about how much farther that would have set us back. Think about how it would have set the timetable back on Satan and all that. Then again you have to go about it in another point of view. You think of it this way with how much time these people had to study to figure it how of how to go ahead and stop the electromagnetic situation that took place and just made it to norm out or whatever the case may be shielded out to where the destruction did not take place.

Now here again according to the Bible this puts us closer towards Armageddon because it is making the confrontation become more at hand as we speak. It is in your face with all that is happening in Jerusalem. But we really don't have a whole lot to worry about until they start having to tear down the Mosque in order to rebuild the Church of God on Temple Mount that was supposedly there originally. Now according to the Bible that is what is supposed to happen with the Muslim temple that was built there. They are going to have to remove it or tear it down in order to build The Church of God there so Satan himself can walk into this building and proclaim himself God. So this situation has to take place according to the Bible. Now here again how far away are we removed from that actually happening in your way of thinking? Was 2012 the resetting of the Christ-Antichrist conflict?

Okay so if that is the case, all that we have to basically ask ourselves what is so dramatic about the 2012 thing that no one even has a philosophy to bring about it? My point is that it goes back to the original thing.

So being here the next new thing about the 2012 event is I believe the extraterrestrials, the Yin and Yang brothers, are trapped here in this electrical time lock of dimension. They are stuck here trying to reach out to go back home. But because these people contaminated us and changed us and made us into their image they have to stay here time locked into this dimension and teach us until we become educated about the extraterrestrials and everything of this nature. Then they will be allowed to go home. These extraterrestrials are the Yin and Yang brothers or good versus evil who are discussed in more detail in another chapter. Okay, so these guys could not go home and they are trapped here in this dimension. I think that it is a matter of really understanding that the extraterrestrials have never really left here. They live with us as an experiment in the DNA which is the Universe all DNA. The Universe all DNA is another chapter. The extraterrestrials live here in the water and in the ground. They can't leave. They have been stalled here and live here because of the destruction they did to themselves on Mars and the fifth planet. So ask yourself, why do they want to stay? In my opinion this is the answer to the 2012 anomaly.

How long did people prepare for 2012? You tell me. There were people who even spent billions of dollars building condominiums in missile silos for safety. So here again do not tell me the rage of safety was among us. So ask yourself, why 2012 did not happen? Why would you believe these serious historians of the past?

Ask yourself how many times would it have taken you to have figured out the solar alignment that had taken place every twenty-six thousand years? How long would it have taken you? We in our lifetime never have figured it out. So who showed us about the stars? The alignment had to have been seen as a constant trouble in time or why would they even have prepared for the devastation that took place. How many times did it take place before they finally realized it and wrote it down for others to share this discovery? Who noticed it first and who advised us to look up into the stars?

It seems as if I am trying to come up with a logical answer to the 2012 anomaly or a scientific answer that scientists will believe and understand. Remember somebody had to show you how to do everything in the beginning. And here you know there is just no answer for why it did not take place. So here again I know this is redundant, but you have got to realize and ask yourself the question. You know why and how there is not another answer to this question. I think that I have solved that. Thank   you.

CHAPTER ELEVEN

THE 2012 ANOMALY

What Happened?

When the December 21, 2012 predicted destruction did not happen it upset me so severely that I wrote this book and had to dig deeper and deeper to find out just what happened.

A coronal mass ejection could have been what was supposed to happen at 2012. One had happened probably twenty- six thousand years earlier. We do not know but it had to happen pretty much the same time over and over again for them to be able to study it and record it and pass it on into history, right?

Now remember that somebody somewhere had to know that in 2012 this coronal mass ejection was going to happen because it happened every twenty-six thousand years. So, we are assuming possibly in the nature of things that each of these planets in our solar system has gone through a coronal mass

178 · GARY STOKES

ejection contamination of being spewed on possibly to cause it to be destroyed. Or is it just every twenty-six thousand years that the coronal mass ejection spews on planet Earth, Mars, and the fifth ring planet and finally destroyed one of them with a perfect shot of coronal mass ejection? Was this mass ejection at 2012 just for the planet Earth this time? You never know when or where the coronal mass ejection will spray on which planet. I still like the idea that the planet Earth is the timer or the clock that initiates when this coronal mass ejection was going to happen.

Also was the planet Earth made to be a time clock so that every twenty-six thousand years the alignment comes around and some way, some reason, somehow, somebody knew that the coronal mass ejection was going to happen and destroy everybody but nobody until 2012 even knew or put their mind around the concept. Yet no one ever understands that the 2012 anomaly was either a twenty-six thousand years cycle or it was the thing of electronic release of the magnetism going through electronical flux or something like that. Just because we do not have the imagination and brains to be able to realize we do not know. If you think about the coronal mass ejection then 2012 was just a spew and everything of that nature that we missed because of the timing was off two or three days or whatever.

You also have to realize that with the 2012 anomaly and this thing called the coronal mass ejection that no one ever really got through to you to say that is just what was going to happen. This coronal mass ejection was supposed to destroy Earth. Does this not seem to you logically that even though we had all the Mayans and others studying this for tens of thousands of years over and over again that, wait a minute, somehow some way somebody knew that this 2012 anomaly thing had to be time oriented where they would know what was going to happen? So the Mayans set up their clock and then from there basically used it as a time clock for when it got back to zero the closest it could to the sun is when the coronal mass ejection happens.

Some way, some reason, somehow, somebody had to know that the coronal mass ejection was going to happen and destroy everybody. But nobody until 2012 even knew or put their mind around the concept. So here again ask yourself would this be enough time for the ancients to be able to see how long it takes the sun to be able to eject or push a planet out. Think about the irony of someone actually being able to pay attention enough to monitor that it is every twenty-six thousand years. In other words it is working longer and lasting longer once it spits the planet out. Anyway, what I am trying to realize and come to grips with is the amount of time it took for someone to know when to pay attention to this. Now in our world being as young as we are we would not know or have privy to any books that would say this is what happens.

Getting back to the 2012 issue. Is there any way we can prove that this kind of event happened before the 2012 event? Is there any scientific way to prove it? I am sure there is a way to prove a coronal mass ejection happened twenty six thousand years earlier than 2012. Now it is just one of those questions I have.

You have to ask if the next coronal mass ejection which is coming up in twenty-six thousand years or whenever will it once again spray upon planet Earth? Or does the coronal mass ejection every twenty-six thousand years have a new position that it sprays upon the planets because they are slowly drifting away from the sun and the coronal mass ejection happens? I do not know if it happens in the same spot or not. It seems logical that as the planet becomes closer to the sun that would initiate some kind of electrical lock, some kind of planetary mass that might allow it to initiate the contact that would allow it to cause a coronal mass ejection and destroy the planets.

What is the situation with the sun and coronal mass ejections now since the 2012 anomaly did not really destroy our planet because it basically got a pass for some reason? Either the extraterrestrials put a pass on it or this is the last time a coronal mass ejection did not have a perfect alignment and missed us. I believe this is probably the proof that the coronal mass ejection missed planet Earth. Either it was earlier or it was later but it did miss us.

Maybe the fifth ring planet which we call the asteroid belt was destroyed so it would change the magnetic anomaly of our solar system to prevent the next 2012 type event from destroying planet Earth. The fifth ring planet might have been destroyed by the oncoming 2012 anomaly which I keep calling the devastation by the alignment at 2012. Maybe the extraterrestrials knew they had to get off their planet and to go someplace else. They had twenty-six thousand years to make the transformation from one planet to another planet because they knew from their past history the anomaly of being destroyed by the wobble every twenty-six thousand years. Well, they could not change it so the only way to change it is to remove the point in which the electricity was being able to focus. In other words, they changed where the wave would go by eliminating the process. If the planet wasn't there, then where did the wave have to travel to the next point of reception? Is that what caused planet Earth to not have the 2012 anomaly this time? It was because the Earth was protected by the moon, the universe all canteen, which forced the beam away and changed the electrical flow of space electricity to shield us instead of destroying us.

Our next question is that if this type of situation had happened at 2012 and hit planet Earth, would it have caused the same type of destruction of breaking planet Earth into little rocks the same as it did to the fifth planet? It is an interesting point of view that the asteroid belt planet was destroyed to stop the magnetic anomaly of the 2012 destruction from ever happening again. This would give the people on those planets twenty-six thousand years to make the transformation to the next planet that was not destroyed by the magnetic pulsation of the 2012 anomaly.

I think this is a very logical perception of understanding. We know it is true that the magnetism and density of the solar system were affected when the asteroid planet was broken up. We do not know when the demise took place but we do know that the asteroid belt rocks are in pieces. No one really wants to say because they do not have the perception to perceive it.

If I am logically correct, then they waited for the 2012 anomaly to not take effect here on planet Earth so they could go forward with their process in the construction of the planet. Therefore, we look at that as if it is an assembly of the Armageddon taking place because the evil was not destroyed for the 2012 anomaly which would have sent evil back into the dark ages.

The fifth planet most likely was destroyed or could have been destroyed in this concept of thought. Imagine being able to change the magnetic situation of the 2012 anomaly by not having a planet there for the energy to bounce off of or take a link out of the chain to where a 2012 type event would not destroy planet Earth in the future like it might have destroyed

CONNECTING THE DOTS IN OUR UNIVERSE · 183

the fifth planet in the past. Therefore when it came time for the 2012 anomaly to happen on planet Earth, the magnetic link had been broken because the fifth planet had been broken up into rubble and could not allow the scientific chain to take place by bouncing energy off of the planet. So, the 2012 anomaly might have been stopped by the destruction of the fifth planet.

So, if the extraterrestrials stopped the 2012 anomaly by destroying the fifth planet, then it would magnetically break the chain so it would not have all the points of distribution for the energy. This would deflect the energy away from planet Earth and not allow the beam to focus and destroy planet Earth like it might have destroyed the fifth planet.

Remember this is just another possibility of how and why the fifth planet was destroyed to come up with a logical reason for why planet Earth was not destroyed by the 2012 anomaly. There have been no reasons given for why the 2012 event did not destroy planet Earth. There were thousands of years of talking and predicting that 2012 would cause some type of destruction to planet Earth. But nobody has given a reason or philosophy why nothing happened to planet Earth at 2012.

Please explain to me why there is nobody else out there that is trying to give a reason why the 2012 event or destruction did not happen. Am I the only one that has the perception that can possibly see this light? If that is the truth then this is my niche and what I am supposed to do.

Are twenty-six thousand years ago the key of when everything started taking place of when the 2012 situation took place, the destruction? Is that the situation that we are talking about here? Is there no other scientific explanation other than the thoughts I have off my head about why 2012 might have been stopped? We do not know what destroyed the fifth planet but it was destroyed. The options I give you for explaining it can only fill in the answers that you have yet to fully understand. So therefore, I know some will say yes and some will say no. But the whole point of view is if I started you to think then you are already halfway home.

It had to have been a magnetic chain lock that they broke when they destroyed the fifth planet. We will not know until we assemble a larger sample of what we assume are the meteors and rocks from the fifth planet into a sphere again and do the mathematical problems of their composition. It might change the gravitational force of how the 2012 event was not supposed to be because if the fifth planet was not there then the next planet to have been destroyed would have been planet Earth. They destroyed the fifth planet themselves so planet Earth would not be destroyed.

So, if you look at the planets where they were at 2012 ask yourself if the fifth planet would have been an important piece of the puzzle to add to the electronic adjustment of the sun not blasting planet Earth but blasting out into space instead? Remember it was said it was altered so it wouldn't hurt planet Earth this time. Now was that a logical statement or did I misunderstand it most likely? But here again the blast did not take place on 2012. It was not blasted towards the Earth. It went somewhere else.

I am trying to say that if the fifth planet was not there, I almost want to think that planet Earth might have been destroyed. I don't see how they would have just destroyed the fifth planet there and go to Earth on the inside and leave all the others out in the rings of our solar system and not destroy them.

When the fifth planet was destroyed it changed the magnetic direction of how 2012 actually took place. Here again the question I ask is, if 2012 took place did it by chance happen to blast towards the fifth planet? And if not, which direction was that blast projected towards? And can we see or perceive any kind of problems in the future because the beam went by us? We missed a chance to harness all that energy into a man-made sphere or an active magnetosphere to basically entrap all that energy that the sun spewed out because we are not educated enough to learn how to fish this space energy from the sun in order to encapsulate it into an energy sphere and then use that energy someplace else. I am asking now is this the same situation that might have made Jupiter what it is?

What if they took the Universe-all canteen and moved it to another place of electronic advantage for them to use because of the 2012 anomaly? They moved it from where it was supposed to bounce off of the fifth planet so it would have been directed here to planet Earth. Or they moved the universe all canteen here to planet Earth in order to stop the direction of it destroying Earth. Instead it destroyed the fifth planet. That might have been what happened before the last 2012 type event that we had.

Do you understand what I am saying with this reapplication of the moon? This gives us a reason for how they can change the space structure of space and stuff. The magnetic wave of space was changed which is what the 2012 anomaly might have originally been. There again is what we are trying to rediscover and figure out.

Just imagine the fifth planet was not destroyed in an earlier 2012 type of event twenty-six thousand years ago by a magnetic destruction because the universe all canteen was there. In this point of view, they destroyed the planet themselves. I believe that is a very logical possibility and would make more sense.

If the sun has these outbursts then the extraterrestrials are smart enough to try to encapsulate this energy and form a planet around that energy. They would store that energy so it is not spewed out all over space and wasted. The extraterrestrials are smart enough to keep it gathered up in some kind of uniform container which allows them to use it to make energy storage pods that are the size of planets.

There again the universe all canteen has a more logical use. It could be used for water or liquids or gas of any nature. Remember it is a canteen. It is a transportation device just like a boxcar on a train or the space shuttle that carries supplies. It is the same thing.

Did they change the electronic path of 2012 by dragging the universe all canteen which we know now is made of aluminum into our orbit? Did they change the destructional direction of 2012 by moving the universe all canteen as I call it the moon? Maybe they are that smart that they can change the electronic direction of space to their advantage.

If they knew they would have to leave the 2012 destruction by the twenty-six thousand years destruction cycle, maybe they knew they had to leave the situation. They took everything with them. They also had the idea that they would possibly be able to go back to that planet and re-inhabit it and re-inhabit Mars such as we are now trying to do as a recolonization process. In other words what we are saying here is that the fifth planet was going to go through the same catastrophic event that planet Earth would have gone through at 2012 and somehow or for some reason they changed the way it didn't happen so they can move back to the planet once the beam got past us. Somehow they knew how to control it. Or it is twenty six thousand years until they have to deal with it again? Maybe now they are trying to move back to Mars because Earth is going to be destroyed.

So, you had twenty-six thousand years to move everybody off the planet Earth back to the planet Mars where Mars wasn't going to be the target of this gamma spray from the sun again. It would only be an intelligent species that would want to go back where they already were from knowing that the damage could not take place in their planet but was going to destroy the Earth this next time around in twenty-six thousand years when it comes up.

CONCLUSION

The Answer to the Questions

Connecting the dots in our universe. How do all these dots fit together or connect to each other? Extraterrestrials, the Yin and Yang brothers, universe all DNA, the sun, coronal mass ejections, the planet Earth, the asteroid belt planet, the universe all canteen, and the 2012 anomaly. How do all of these seemingly different things fit together? How do all these dots connect?

A summation or an answer to all of the questions: I believe the reason the extraterrestrials are here is because they destroyed their planet and had to leave it. They came to planet Earth because it just happened to be a perfect place because it was not too hot or too cold. The Yin and Yang brothers are two extraterrestrials who are troublemakers and are trapped here on planet Earth and are not able to go home. They are trapped here to have to grow us up and to be babysitters to us because of what they did. I believe that they did what I call the unforgivable sin which was they changed our DNA and they stole our planet. That is what I believe. So if they changed our DNA and made us into their image, did they not take over the planet where we were living as well? Yes, they did. They transferred themselves from the fifth planet. These two guys demised and beat themselves up so much that they destroyed their own planet. When they destroyed their own planet they had to leave and go someplace else.

The Wall of Humanity at Puma Punku in Bolivia has over forty carved stone figureheads of various races or species of all of the different types of extraterrestrials that have been here and probably shared their DNA. The stone figureheads are there to represent the extraterrestrials' science of their DNA to show that they created all these different species through the DNA that they manufactured. The extraterrestrials that came here stole our planet, changed our DNA, and changed us from what we would have become to what we are now. They are the ones who changed our DNA and made us what we are now. We are all just a science project.

I believe that the extraterrestrials created the sun to produce the planets. The sun to me is the mother that birthed all the planets. It was created to get hot to produce and create the planets which were eventually put in orbit out there. The sun is the world's largest forge in the sky and is the hugest oven that produced the planets and the elements in the planets. The planets were produced as mining facilities to be harvested by the extraterrestrials coming by and mining from them whatever they thought they needed from that planet.

The sun was so hot and had so much extra material inside that it had a coronal mass ejection and spit out a planet or birthed a planet to start the solar system. The sun ejected each planet as a coronal mass ejection. The sun shot the farthest planet out first and it had a chance to start cooling for twenty-six thousand years. That one planet could have started the solar system. If we are correct then every twenty-six thousand years the sun went through the process of having a coronal mass ejection and producing another planet.

There is no logical reason for the fifth planet to have been destroyed into pieces unless the extraterrestrials who lived there did it. What they are actually telling us is that these two new guys, the Yin and Yang brothers, destroyed their own planet. We are assuming that they destroyed their planet into rocks and pieces during some type of war with each other. I believe it was an ongoing event that the Yin and Yang brothers had because neither one of them wins. So that leads us to believe the extraterrestrials once lived on the fifth planet but destroyed the planet and then moved away to planet Earth.

Planet Earth was created with all of its minerals to be a huge mining project. The planet Earth could be nothing more than a huge mining colony facility that provides goods for everybody else in the rest of the solar system as well as other dimensions. They are harvesting all of the chemicals and minerals from inside the planet. The planet was created with all of its minerals to be a huge mining project. The extraterrestrials had to heat up the planet Earth so they could put a motor inside of it and then after it was hot enough they had to cool it down with the water that they brought with them in the universe all canteen. The extraterrestrials came to live here on planet Earth so they could mine it.

You have to realize that there was no water on the planet Earth until the extraterrestrials brought the water with them in the universe all canteen. The reason we call it the universe all canteen is because it is the only way you could bring so much water with you if you destroyed your planet and had to move to a new planet? You are going to have to have a place to pour it into and leave it in reserve in the moon up above. Remember these two warring factions have just destroyed their planet from years of warring so basically they have to have a way to take all the water with them that they could.

Okay, you say that you understand all this about the extraterrestrials, the Yin and Yang brothers, universe all DNA, the sun, coronal mass ejections, planet Earth, the asteroid belt, and the universe all canteen or the moon but how does the 2012 anomaly connect to this? Well, let me connect that dot to the others.

We just happened to have the other energy source in the planet Earth that might create the magnetic lock that I was talking about earlier to release the 2012 coronal mass ejection. This is because its energy is a gravity that is created on the planet Earth that activates with the sun being closest to the Earth. In other words, when the thing that gives us gravity all the time comes to a point at twenty-six thousand years is very possibly the generation motor that generates and creates gravity on Earth. This generation motor just happens to release the electrical lock towards the sun which allows the sun to release a coronal mass ejection.

My theory of this and why the planet Earth might not have gotten sprayed at 2012 is because just possibly the coronal mass ejection might have been at a weaker state and therefore either was too slow to hit Earth and it went past us or it was too fast and it went past us on the other side. But either way you go the Earth was not hit by a coronal mass ejection at 2012.

Now wouldn't it be funny if the extraterrestrials blocked the coronal mass ejection from actually taking place and diverted the spray someplace else. In other words how did they interfere with the gravity on the Earth to finally stop the coronal mass ejection from taking place? Now if they can move these huge hundred ton rocks like they are nothing with this gravitational force that they have then wouldn't it be a neat science project to go to the next step to see if you could stop the coronal mass ejection from destroying the planet that you had created. Their planet had been destroyed by an earlier coronal mass ejection which caused them to flee to planet Earth. Then they had twenty- six thousand years to figure out the cycle on how to stop the coronal mass ejection from destroying their new home planet. Well it sounds logical to me.

It is almost as if we have created our purely and only yin and yang thing by creating the sun and the twenty-six thousand years wobble and cycle that we had no idea would be our undoing. It is a strange sort of comeback in the way of doing that when the sun goes supernova it will destroy all the planets in the solar system so they can start the process all over again. Gravity becomes the triggering device every twenty-six thousand years when it approaches the special alignment with the sun. Not knowing that they created it must have really bothered them. When they did it is the same on all the other solar systems everywhere the sun exists.

The ones that created the planet Earth did not know when they created gravity they were creating the igniting sequence or the triggering device that actually allowed the 2012 thing to take place. In other words when they created gravity on the planet Earth they also created a way for the sun to have the ability to release an electrical lock. It is like someone reached out with a vibrational gun and released the electric lock waves just like we do when we move one hundred ton rocks. The funny part is that when we created gravity we possibly could have created our own demise by not realizing that when we make gravity on a planet it also is an electrical release from the sun to dump its contents. That is sort of a funny way of a true yin and yang.

The real thing is I wonder if all the other solar systems are already privy to this which I am sure that they are. This is true on every event that has this situation. It is unique that our solar system study through the Mayans and everybody else in any of the other solar systems should have known this same scenario would have to exist if everything works out magnetically for the planet producing gravity to release some kind of electrical lock from the sun.

In my opinion now as I see it the Yin and Yang brothers are still living among us and are almost ready to try to cause the same demise here on planet Earth as they did on Mars and the fifth planet.

In my opinion Armageddon is being forced upon us because of what happened in 2012 because no destruction occurred on December 21, 2012. We can only look into the future to know when the time is upon us. It seems dark now but just remember what they have told us. This cannot happen until the original Church of God has been rebuilt in Israel so Satan can walk inside and proclaim himself God. This time seems to be far off in our future due to the fact that the Muslim mosque occupies the exact same spot. Oh, what turmoil this should produce! So stay conscious and watch for the signs to best prepare for all of us.

With me being able to connect the dots, I hope this will answer some of your questions and give you a direction to think on. Maybe this book will give you some kind of logical conclusion to the events of who we are, where we came from, and why we are here. In my opinion the Yin and Yang brothers educated us enough to be greeted in the extraterrestrial world of the beyond and then and only then will they be released and be able to journey on their way back home.

In summation, I hope this book will give you some closure on who we are, what did they change in our DNA, and was this the original sin that made them become electrically time locked here until the return of the Christ versus the Antichrist.

It has taken me a lifetime of experiences and thousands of hours of research to hit on those points that I call the dots. Basically, this is nothing more than being able to step back from the initial view and let common logic tell you what the truth is. This is only one opinion and one conclusion from every one of us who have thought of the beyond.

So the basic thing we are trying to realize and understand

is this, why can't we seem to put these dots together anymore? How come I seem to put these dots together and nobody else does? Maybe it is because I am supposed to do it in this book. But anyway, the whole point of view is to always to deduce things down to the essence and ask the question. When you get to the essence if you do not know the answer and you stop, then you will never have the answer because you have not learned to think about it long enough and deep enough to ask the next question that might open you up to the truth that unlocks ten thousand pages of information that you see and desire in the future. Such things are only in our imagination to come true and if we pay it forward and see it forward, then the secret is to see it, imagine it, feel it, and own it. Then if I started you to think, guess what my friends, you are halfway home.

Remember I do not say I have the answer. I say this is a possibility of the answer. It is more or less like a logical answer question type of thing. What do you believe, how do you think? So, the basis of it is different than mine of how you came to understand your basis of this. Let's compare and understand this problem in space that people walk away from because I guess they do not have the time or perception or depth of thought or connection to understand it as deep as I do right now.

I am not a scientist or anybody that studies science. This is just my opinion as an individual educated person on the topic. I am an independent study person. I do it for my own entertainment and I am trying to share what I believe is accurate and everybody else would like to know on the easy side of it. I call that being able to pick up a book and read it to make a summarized version of the last twelve or fifteen years of my life. Just think of it that way. But anyway, as you go through time it is funny how you have to step back and look at how you have spent the past years. You have to realize and understand sometimes and just step back to see the larger picture. You never know when you see the complete picture because it is very seldom that we do. May God bless you with the ability to connect the dots in our universe so you can see the light.

ABOUT THE AUTHOR

Gary Stokes calls himself a question and answer man who likes to make people think. He is an idea man and a creator and is independently educated. He and his wife Carolyn live in Powder Springs, GA. Visit his website at:

https://garystokes.com

.